Metaphorosis

September 2019

Beautifully made speculative fiction

Also from Metaphorosis Books

Score – an SFF symphony

Reading 5X5: Readers' Edition
Reading 5X5: Writers' Edition

Best Vegan Science Fiction & Fantasy

Best Vegan SFF of 2018
Best Vegan SFF of 2017
Best Vegan SFF of 2016

Metaphorosis Magazine

Metaphorosis: Best of 2018
Metaphorosis: Best of 2017
Metaphorosis: Best of 2016

Metaphorosis 2018: The Complete Stories
Metaphorosis 2017: The Complete Stories
Metaphorosis 2016: Nearly Complete Stories

Monthly issues

by B. Morris Allen

Susurrus
Allenthology: Volume I
Tocsin: and other stories
Start with Stones: collected stories
Metaphorosis: a collection of stories

Metaphorosis

September 2019

edited by
B. Morris Allen

Metaphorosis Books

Neskowin

ISSN: 2573-136X (online)
ISBN: 978-1-64076-147-6 (e-book)
ISBN: 978-1-64076-148-3 (paperback)

September 2019

Some Sun and Delilah

B. Morris Allen

"I'll cut your hair," she said impulsively one evening. "You're getting shaggy, and far too blond with all this sun."

We were vacationing in the islands, trusting the fresh sea winds to bring life to stale hopes. We sat half-naked on limestone dust as soft as flour, and sifted it through our fingers. We'd made love as many times as there were shells strewn on the sand. It had brought back our glory days, when I was strong and confident, she sleek and clever. In our quiet cove under coconut palms, with the sly serenade of tropical wavelets tickling our feet, the heat fanned no flames, only set them flickering and uncertain, my small supply of virility too quickly exhausted, too slowly replenished. After only two days, happy banter ebbed with the sea, swirling away with manta rays and parrot fish to leave only silence and doubt and desperate measures.

She'd cut my hair only two weeks since, in the shabby Nairobi hotel that marked the start of our adventure of rediscovery. "To make the local girls jealous," she'd said at the time.

"Sure, why not?" I searched for a joke to match her mood. "Transform me to a handsome itinerant, searching out island rhythms."

"I'll show you island rhythms," she said, brushing one small, bikini-clad breast against my shoulder. "After your haircut."

In a chair on the porch of our bayside hotel cottage, I was hers to direct, to shape. "You're feeding stereotypes," I called as she gathered her tools. "Woman caring for man."

"As are you," she said. "Cave man with no couth." She pointed with her chin. "Wet your hair and come back."

A quick rinse later, I sat on the porch, cool water dripping down my thin, bare chest as she busied herself with scissor and comb. Little scraps of washed-out gold lay in shoals on my slightly sunburnt belly, and fell in clusters on her rich mahogany arms.

"I've been thinking," she said at last.

"Always good."

She folded my ear a little harder than I liked, and I winced at the thought of cartilage crumpling.

"I was talking with Angele, earlier." Angele and Pierre were the Rwandan couple to the left, our only neighbours aside from the Ukrainians who fought all night and spent their days in separate silence. I could see Yuri now, still out in his kayak in the bay, matching the hours of peace to the hours of light.

"Find anything out?" Angele was far younger than Pierre, and Rwandans were unlikely tourists so far from the mainland.

"She's his assistant, and they're on a study trip, investigating local government structures."

"Oh, come on." I took advantage of a break in the snipping to look around at Del. "Surely you don't believe that." We heard them having sex often enough, with a frequency and duration that gave us both food for thought.

"That's her story. He's the Deputy Minister, apparently." She stepped behind me and pushed my head forward. "Anyway, that's not the point. Angele said there's a guide who does a nice tour of local historical spots." She traded her scissors for a safety razor and scraped my tender, salt-crusted skin. "I thought we might check it out tomorrow."

Island history was low on my list of interests, but keeping Del happy was high. "Sure. Why not?"

"Apparently the hotel can set it up. If you don't want to, though, maybe we can go kayaking tomorrow." She stepped back to assess her handiwork. "Or you can go with Yuri."

I smiled as dashingly as I could. "I don't know. Historical tour with beautiful brunette all to myself, or vigorous exercise with bulky Ukrainian gangster. Hard choice."

"I'm serious," she said. "If you don't want to come..." I could see that it was important to her, that she was trying as hard as I to avoid those awkward silences, the long moments of broken conversation between bouts of sex.

"I do," I assured her with a kiss on the hand. "And thanks for the haircut. What did you say happens afterward?" I drew her down toward me and kissed her sun-flaked lips before taking her inside to make her happy.

In the morning, we rose early for a quick swim in the shallow bay, threading through the beds of seaweed, trying to avoid encountering the little sharks more frightened than we, and the stingrays hiding under the sand. A game of tag turned quickly into a clinging, fumbling roll, and we sped back to shore and bed. Sex was best early in the day, when it was still fresh, when our hopes sprang newborn from dreams of glad repletion.

After she came, we lay for a while together, my hand still trapped in the warmth between her legs, my face resting on her shoulder.

"So," I said when she sighed and stirred at last. "How do we find this guide lady?" I'd thought of pretending ignorance, letting her, sated, ignore the plan. But she'd been sated other mornings also, as well as I could manage.

She smiled and rolled to face me. "I'm so glad you remembered." She laid an arm on my chest. "I know it's not really your thing, but I thought ..." She'd apparently thought something too dangerous to name, and changed it mid-sentence. "You know. New places, new things."

"Old historical sites." It was a joke, though, and we showered together, soaping each other in silent search of a resurgence that didn't arrive.

"Just as well," she said, rinsing. "I told the hotel we'd meet her at ten." I looked at my watch. We had just enough time to dress. I carefully didn't consider when she might have had time to arrange the meeting.

At the oversized thatched hut that served as reception, our guide was waiting. She was small and a pleasant light brown, with tightly curled grey hair, and faintly Asian eyes that widened when she saw us. Better prospects than she'd envisioned, perhaps.

"Bonjour," I said in my best rusty French. "Parlez-vous anglais?"

"Of course, monsieur. I am an accredited guide. Your French is excellent, but we can speak English if you prefer."

"Of course we'll speak English," Del decided. "He's just showing off." She extended a hand. "My name is Del."

"Mine is Carinne. And this must be Sam." Her right eye, on the far side from Del, winked at me. "You see? I do my research as well. The owner here is an old friend."

We spent the morning touring plain, whitewashed churches and research stations, squat municipal buildings and decrepit statues. Despite Carinne's best efforts, I was bored, and I doubt Del was more enthralled, but we persevered until the tour ended on a narrow tarmac street with open air cafés and restaurants to one side, fine white sand to the other.

"Here I leave you," declared Carinne. "At the best restaurant for you on the island." She gestured to one of the indistinguishable restaurants, its white plastic tables stained and scored by years of careless diners.

"Thank you, Carinne. It's very kind, but ... we're vegetarians. Very strict." Seaside places, in my experience, serve fish, fish, and more fish.

"I told you, Mr. Sam. I do my research. The proprietor here serves the best vegetarian meals in town." That twinkle again. "Perhaps the only ones. He is my good friend, and you may trust him. Now come," she ushered us through a gap in the low whitewashed wall. "Jean! Les étrangers ont arrives. Apporte les aliments exotiques." She smiled at me.

"But you must join us, Carinne," said Del.

"No, Ms. Del. I cannot. It is very kind, of course, but ..."

"Never mind that," Del insisted. *Why not?* I thought. Carinne had done her best, and I didn't grudge her a little extra. It might help us avoid the awkwardness of a tip, and I gave Del silent credit for the idea.

The food was excellent — grilled vegetables, a salad of seaweed and beans, and a spicy curry of coconut milk and nuts poured over rice. Jean, the rail-thin black proprietor and cook, bustled merrily back and forth with dishes, pickles, and drinks, until at last Del insisted he join us as well.

We told abbreviated versions of our lives, and listened to their talk of island scandal, until, bellies bulging, we sat back, vainly trying to find room for delicious little cups of some white jelly, with bits of mango. It tasted of coconut and mint.

"So," asked Jean at last. "How was your tour?"

I tried desperately to remember the names of even one of the sites.

Del, more self-assured, said "The churches were lovely."

"Bah," said Jean. "The usual spots. Is this the best you can do, Carinne?"

She shrugged. "This is the tour. I am sorry if it is not interesting."

"Not at all," I said hurriedly.

Jean cut me off. "No one is interested in these things."

"It was very interesting," I insisted. "The botanical research station, for example, where they're growing the, um, ..."

"Coco de mer," offered Del. The nut looked somewhat like a woman's buttocks from one side, and the other side looked even less like a woman's front.

Jean sniffed. "For tourists. They love it. The nut has no uses, otherwise."

"It makes good bowls," offered Carinne. "And the jelly from young nuts is very good." She gestured at the dessert bowls before us.

"And it's an aphrodisiac," Jean admitted.

"Where can we get more?" I jumped in, joking.

"Very rare," Carinne said, shaking her head. "Jean has been generous with you."

"I give my guests what they need," he said. Did I imagine a sympathetic glance in my direction? "What about you?" He caught Carinne's eye and held it.

"Me." It was clear that she knew what he meant.

"Yes, you. Why not show them something really interesting, for once?" The weight of a hidden message was not lost on any of us.

Carinne considered, looking from me to Del to the dessert with a troubled brow.

"Why not, Carinne?" Del asked. "Is there more to show us? Please do."

"Are you sure?" She looked searchingly into Del's eyes. "Perhaps. But you," she turned her keen gaze to me. "What is it you long for?"

"Something new," I said glibly. "Or old." In truth, another day of boring monuments was not my idea of a holiday, but clearly the mystery had caught Del's interest, and for that, I was willing to spend a few more dull hours growing blisters. Plus, we might end up here for lunch again, and that seemed an excellent idea.

Carinne bit her lip, but Jean nodded, and she gave in. "Very well. Tomorrow afternoon, then. There is a temple. It is very old, very broken. You may not find it interesting."

A temple, at least, would be a break from cinder block administrative buildings, and equally stolid churches.

"It sounds lovely," said Del. "Tomorrow, then,"

Del and I left Carinne at the restaurant, and walked slowly, happily down the narrow streets to our hotel. We were silent, mostly, but we held hands, and for the first time in a while, it felt good.

That night, it felt more than good. I managed twice times, three times — a record! Then four and five, before we sank exhausted into sleep. In the morning, we were sore but willing, and after slow, tender lovemaking, we spent the early day drowsing and snuggling as we hadn't done for months. After a perfunctory lunch, we moved to the open air bar, and sat drinking cool, fresh juice until Carinne arrived.

"You are ready?" she asked.

"Ready," Del declared for the two of us.

"Ready," I echoed, remembering the night. "Ready. And maybe dinner at Jean's, eh?"

Carinne shook her head, serious. "Perhaps. But too much coco de mer… It is not good for everyone. Maybe not for you." Was my inadequacy so clearly on display for all to see? I bridled, but Carinne put her hand on my arm. "It is no bad thing," she said. "The more one takes, the higher the price." I was unsure if she referred to the law of supply and demand, or some metaphysical mumbo jumbo, but her eyes were kind, and I chose to let it go.

"Let's be off, then," I said to cover my irritation. "Ruined temples, here we come."

We set out on foot, up the main road into the coastal hills. I insisted on carrying Carinne's bag full of supplies, and she handed it over with a shrug — a peace offering of sorts, perhaps; a nod to my virility.

We turned off the road to a broad path, then a narrow one, then a faint trail in the jungle. Around us, lianas hung from jellyfish trees and palms.

"Look," said Del, pointing to the side. "Coco de mer." Indeed, they grew more frequent the further we went, until we stood in a veritable forest of palms.

"So much for rarity," I said. "Maybe we can point Jean to this place." Del reached back to squeeze my hand.

Soon after, the trail debouched into a small clearing with a short drop to the beach one side, and rock on the other. On the inland side, a single stained stone pillar poked drunkenly toward the sky.

"Temple, I'm guessing," I offered, to fill the silence. It didn't look like much. There was the one pillar, a few tumbled blocks, and a curtain of vines. There was no sign of a portico or roof; just the remains of these stones.

"Is there an inside?" Del asked. Without waiting for an answer, she strode over to the ruins.

Beside the single pillar, vines hid not rock, but a dank, dismal emptiness. It smelled of urine, dust, and guano.

"After you," I motioned to Carinne, before remembering that if there were torches to be found, they must be in her pack, still tight against my back. Del had already plunged into the darkness, though, and Carinne stepped in after her.

"Give me your hand," she said, reaching forward for Del's and back for mine. I took it, not wanting to let them head off without me into the dark. There was a small delay as she pushed ahead of Del, and we all traded hands.

As my eyes adjusted to the dim light, I saw that the entry was lined with rough stone slabs, and looked up with trepidation to see the same just over my head. "Is it safe?" I asked, scuffing the toe of my shoe into the silt of the floor.

"Safe?" asked Carinne, starting forward again. "I think we are past safe."

"What? What the...?"

"Oh, man up, Sam. It's just a little darkness."

I bit down on my response and shuffled forward, my shoes sliding past unknown objects as we twisted and turned into a tunnel. Probably the bones of small animals. Or of unmanly men, frightened of the dark.

"Oh," exclaimed Del from before me. A moment later, I could see a faint grey glow from walls that seemed to stretch far higher than before. "It's beautiful," she said. "Like pearls."

"Very dirty pearls," I said, telling myself to enjoy her pleasure, but unable to make myself do it.

In the dim light, I could see her shake her head at this evidence of philistine character, but she said nothing.

The glow grew stronger, and I could see that it came from a coarse white coating high on the walls.

"Like mother of pearl," Del said, though I could see no such resemblance.

Now that there was light, however faint, I could see that the walls had changed from stone slabs to raw stone, scraped and broken in places to widen the passage. Stalactites dripped down from the ceiling, or formed veins down the walls. It formed a sort of natural temple in itself, and I wondered why it wasn't better known. It was certainly a better tourist attraction than the dumpy town hall.

At the far end of this natural hall, we entered another tunnel. It was short; after only two quick turns, we emerged into the blinding outdoor light. My eyes slowly, painfully adjusted, to see a lush, green paradise of fruit and flowers. I felt a sense of discontinuity, as if I'd stepped into an entirely different world. Not dark and close, like the thick palms of the outer island, this land was light and open, with lawns of moss, and benches of smooth stone shaded by broad yellow blossoms on tall, pale stalks.

Half-hidden by leaves, like a mixer at god's nudist colony, group upon group of beautiful people. Young, old, fat, thin, pale, dark, but all with an ineffable sense of grace, an almost tangible aura of perfection. They were people you just wanted to be with, full of smiles and warmth and a twinkle in the eyes.

Del was already among them, chatting, shaking hands, being hugged — a friend among old friends she'd only just met. I watched with stupefaction as she passed among them, casually shedding bits of clothing as she went. A hat here, a shoe here, handing off her blouse as if it were the most natural thing in the world. By the time she was naked, she was hidden by the crowd. I yearned to go to her, half envious, half jealous, held back by fear and, I slowly realized, by Carinne's hand in mine. Slowly, unwillingly, I looked toward her.

Our guide stood just inside the cave. In contrast to perfection, she seemed a crumpled gargoyle of nut-brown parchment and angled bone. With one gnarled clutch of twigs, she held close to the rough stone of the rock face, as if mooring herself against a winter storm. Her fragile form seemed now a caricature of delicacy, a mockery of beauty drawn by the cruelest of artists, a satirist of poise and elegance.

"Stay," she said, pulling on my hand with her own frail fingers. "Stay. This is not for you."

I stared at her, uncomprehending. Here was Eden recreated, Shangri-La amidst the ocean, Arcadia discovered and Pan no doubt among the crowd. Making love to my own love, no doubt.

"Let her go," Carinne said. "She will come back."

I shook my head and pulled away, stepped out into the warm and gentle sun.

"Stay," she called again, her voice thin and harsh and bereft of all command. "You will regret it."

It could have been Cassandra's catchphrase, for all the attention anyone has ever paid those words. I turned away to follow Del, to join or rescue her.

I stepped toward the nearest of the golden people, a short, plump man with skin so black it shone like obsidian, and a woman blonde as gold and twice as bright. They smiled and took me in their arms. I felt a man among men, with hands as strong as oak and capable of any task. We walked arm in arm among the crowd. I spoke with the flowing eloquence of my best moments, said the right things at the right times, never stumbled, never lost for words. The men looked up to me, respected me. The women pressed against me, fluttered their eyes, laughed at my jokes, rejoined with cutting repartee always clever, never cruel. We competed amongst each other, and I won as many matches as I lost, all in good grace, all in good spirits. When we made love, it was a natural consequence, the graceful conclusion of one impish contest or another. When it was over, there were no hidden glances, no bitter, unsatisfied looks, only utter contentment, and a fluid shift to other topics, other activities. We talked, we laughed, we sang. We ate fruit sweet and tart and refreshing all at once, drank the milk of coconuts, or water as pure as the sky was blue. It lasted forever.

In every tale, forever has an end, the moment when the infinity of now becomes contained, forced back from eternity by the boundaries of tomorrow and of yesterday.

One day, or night, or dawn, as we composed eddas on the stars and moon and sun, a woman curled in between a male form and a female one, lay across a lap, soft breasts against soft thigh. She looked at me with warm eyes of jade, and smiled. I lost my place, but the crowd carried on, taking my long verse for its own, continuing and reshaping it, making my stumble into a victory.

"Hello, Sam," she said.

"Del." I knew her now, and though she shone with the grace of all these other gods, she was the same.

"Are you happy, Sam?" She reached out and stroked my hair. "At last?"

And though I had sung of happiness moments before, of a sudden I was not. I was cold and stiff and dry, and fear pressed in on me.

"Let's go home," she said. As if home were more than bills and work and strain and a squalid flat.

I heard her cry behind me as I ran, the click of my bones setting the metre for the sound of my name, repeated over and over in diminishing echoes. I plunged through a crowd of strangers, in search of contentment. I lost myself in women, holding them in brief, brutish spasms that left me drained and empty, left them frowning as they turned away in search of other partners. The men took me in, shook my hands with grips that made me wince, talked in codes I was always slow to decode, turned me away for better companions. I slaked my thirst with water that tasted of silt, ate green fruit already riddled with rot. At last I slept.

When I woke, my thoughts were slow and painful, and my mouth tasted of decay. I stretched in painful jerks. Beneath me, sharp corners of flint gouged loose skin, sent flurries of gravel down to the muddy rill below. Above me on either side stretched crags of stone hung with scraggly bushes. And when I rose, not far away, Carinne and Del watching with compassion and contempt.

I gathered my clothing, torn and scattered among the jagged boulders of the ravine, fished one shoe from a puddle, the other from a thornbush. As I dressed, the women chatted quietly until at last I stood before them, the barest semblance of a man.

We spoke little as we traversed the tunnels, Carinne's torch leading the way. She carried her own pack. I took Del's hand in the grand central chamber, and she let it hang there, limp and distant until we came once more to the dark, salty night of the exit. There, she squeezed once and let go. We walked home in silence, letting Carinne go her way with no more than a nod.

We kept apart for the remaining days of our vacation. Some days, I went out with Yuri and his kayaks. Some days Del did. On those days I sat alone on our little porch, overlooking the sea. Yuri's pretty brunette came by once or twice, but when I didn't respond, she left me alone. Pierre and I talked, sometimes, but I knew little about African politics, and he had little else to say.

I went back to the temple, of course. When Del was out, or early in the morning, or late at night. You know what I found. Sometimes nothing. Sometimes the cave had no exit, sometimes no entrance. Sometimes it was a den of dust and dry bone. Once it was full of island hooligans who beat me and robbed me and threw me to the beach below the cliff. When I crawled home at last, Del said nothing, only bandaged my wounds with quick efficiency, and went to take tea with Angele.

I spoke with Carinne one more time, at Jean's little restaurant. She just shook her head. "It was for Del," she said. "It was suited to her. A dream and a release.

For people like you it is only danger and obsession and ruin."

I told Del those words, and she shrugged. "You hold too closely, Sam. You're a man of infatuations." She took my hand gently, looked me in the eye as she cut her losses. "Be happy, Sam. Next time."

After we left the islands, we didn't see each other again. She took her things from my flat, and I didn't search her out. I had moments of sorrow, moments of rage, of violence. The other tenants, cowards all, asked that my lease not be renewed. I left the landlord my wreck of a home, and moved.

Here in the north, the waves are tall and cruel, and the beach is cold black grit. Hard work has made me strong, too strong. I lay my head upon the sand, and it mingles with my long, graying hair. When I comb it out, the sand forms stiff, crumbling patterns on my hearth, mountains and canyons of piled, isolated grains, touching but ever separate. I throw them in the fire, but they never melt into glass. Tomorrow, though, I will turn up the heat. I will comb my hair and wear my best clean clothes. I will go to the town, and sit in the library or the teahouse or the pub, and I will try to make a friend. If the gods are with me, I will see whether strength can build as well as destroy.

See B. Morris Allen's story "Some Sun and Delilah" online at Metaphorosis.
If you liked it, leave a comment. Authors love that!
Remember to subscribe to our e-mail updates so you'll know when new stories are posted.

About the story

I wanted to write a story in the style of Richard Cowper (John Murry), and was specifically inspired by his novelette "Incident at Huacaloc", about a couple who visit an old temple with troubling results. I stole those elements and some of the feel of the story, though the rest is quite different. I don't remember now whether I already had the title lying around or it came long with the idea. I seldom address sex in my stories, but here I made it central to the narrator's sense of self. Details of the temple itself are invented, but the general location draws vaguely from a wonderful trip to the Seychelles many years ago when we lived in central Africa and figured it was as close as we'd ever get. Sadly, the vegetarian food wasn't as good as in the story. And I don't recall the coco de mer having any effect. But the snorkeling was beautiful.

Cowper's story "Incident at Huacaloc" was first published in F&SF in October 1981, and later collected in *The Tithonian Factor and Other Stories*.

Favorites from Here and Abroad

Peter T. Donahue

Two giant polyps were nibbling at the husk of a shopping mall some miles off. I was focused on a sludge-tower, though, just a half mile down the hill from me. I'd have to pass it. From where I stood, on the street that zig-zagged down to the basin of the valley, I couldn't see the tower's base. A ridge, wearing a row of rotting condo roofs like an epaulet, was in the way.

For a second I wished my brother were with me. That I hadn't ditched him in the raspberry thicket. He had a map in his head, and could close his eyes and find a route to any place in the valley. All I could do was memorize what happened where.

I felt something tapping at my ankle, and looked down. A mouse. With her small pink hand, she gestured at me. Wanted me to stoop down.

"Princess Tuuli," she said. Her voice was quiet.

"Hello, Dokka," I replied, crouching lower.

"I'm surprised to find you alone in this place," continued Dokka. She twitched nervously, and flicked her ears, trying on the movements and manners of a mouse. Dokka had been many things, she told me, to see what each was like.

"There's a house the polyps have passed over," I told her. "I heard it's full of books." I couldn't hold in my broad smile.

"But where is your brother?"

"Banjoko? Off by the raspberry patch, waiting for a courier drone. I gave him the slip."

"He will be angry."

"I had to!" I argued. The mouse winced, and I lowered my voice. "Banjoko won't leave the drop-point until the drone gets there, but the sun is going down. I had to break one rule or the other."

Dokka knew what I meant. Momsatu had two rules for her foster children: stick together, be home before dark. The mouse was unconvinced.

"Don't worry," I said. "Banjoko will get over it when I come back with an armload of new science books."

"Very well. But mind the dangers of the valley, Princess."

"There's only the one sludge-tower, Dokka, and it's sleepy and slow. It's shutting down for the night, see?" I pointed, and Dokka acknowledged that the living skyscraper had barely moved in the last few minutes. Sludge-creatures reminded me of trolls in the old folktales, but in reverse: turning to stone at sunset instead of sunrise. I zipped up my hoodie. I had to get moving.

"Anyway, it will probably stay in the basin," I added. "Banjoko says sludge-towers don't like to waste energy climbing hills. And I think the house is on the near side of that ridge. I'll be safe."

Dokka shook her head. "The arcs," she said.

"Well, you're right," I conceded. "I'll have to be careful about that." The solid sludge-towers, like this one, didn't glom stuff like the more wispy polyps did. But sometimes, as they shut down, they grew buds that shot huge arcs of lightning.

Some said polyps were like sheep, and sludge-towers more like shepherds. Banjoko argued polyps and sludgers were more like different appendages of the same giant creature. Both formed in downdrafts from the sky-web, the layer of sooty strands up in the atmosphere. High up where, the grown-ups insisted, only clouds should be. And somehow, living in the filaments of the sky-web, was the upper world. Everyone had a different name for it. I called it Sky Island, from a story I read. Momsatu called it 'cyberspace, or whatever'; she was never sure she had the right word. Uncle Hrithik called it *Parama padam* when he was drunk, and noetic space when he was sober. Most people just called it up there, or the world above. Dokka was from there.

And that's where my birth family had gone.

Dokka and I said goodbye, and I headed down into the valley. I jogged where I could. Mostly I had to clamber over places where the pavement was cracked and jumbled (a polyp had torn up the street years ago, looking for fiber optic cables).

I came to a fork and couldn't decide. Left or right? Cave, my sister Magda's man, had discovered the house and told my uncle about it over coffee. My ears perked up, of course, and I tried to memorize the route he described. But he used street names I didn't know. The polyps liked aluminum, and had glommed all the street signs before I moved here.

That ridge with the condo garden was to my right. Just behind it, only a few blocks away, the sludge-tower was still catching rose-gold sunlight on its upper third, while the rest of the valley was starting to get blue and dusky. I was realizing this wouldn't be a fifteen minute trip, after all.

I felt the wind change, and goosebumps prickled all over my body. As I rubbed my arms, I noticed patches of soot on my hoodie sleeves changing texture. The particles of graphene were writhing, standing on end like iron filings reacting to a magnetic field. These were not good signs. I looked up.

The sludge tower was forming a bud, like a gall on a gigantic tree trunk. I thought, *I am about to be struck by lightning.*

My mind went blank with panic.

But, in the next moment, a starling swooped down from its perch on an old utility pole.

"This way, Princess Tuuli," she said. It was Dokka again, in a new body. She called me Princess so I could always recognize her.

She fluttered and darted up the street that branched left. I followed, running hard to put distance between myself and the tower. I felt my hair starting to stand up, and I frantically pulled it down. As if that would protect me.

A flash of light. Thunder. It didn't hit me, but it felt close.

The bird led me towards a park. A large one, with different types of dead trees.

"Under here," called Dokka.

I followed her through a stand of skeletal pines. I ducked under branches, felt them scratch my face. An abandoned playground opened in front of me.

The floor of tire scraps was heaved up everywhere by saplings. Paper birch, black locust, ailanthus, sassafras. Dokka flitted from tree to tree, showing me a path to a clearing. Finally, next to the rotted, wooden stumps of a former jungle gym, I found a patch of rubbery ground and plopped myself down. Clever Dokka—rubber was an insulator.

Another sky-tearing flash and rumble.

"Will the tower come after me?" I asked Dokka, panting. My lungs hurt.

She had settled on the branch of a dead sassafras. She quietly chattered and purred, trying on the manners of a starling. After a moment she said, "No, Princess. You are safe."

I collapsed, kicking up a puff of the ever-present soot. As I coughed a little and caught my breath, I stared up, and watched the drifting threads of the sky-web. Like the top of the tower, the web caught the pink light of the setting sun.

"The Kingdom of the Pinks," I said, remembering the plot of *Sky Island*. I calmed down, and turned to smile at Starling-Dokka.

"My guardian angel," I said.

"Ha. If you like," said the bird. "That book-filled house you spoke of—are you close?" she asked.

"I think so."

She abruptly turned to me, and said, "Well, this was fun. Goodbye."

"Wait!" I said, but it was too late. The starling dropped off the branch, dead.

I watched as a bubble formed from the graphene caked on the skinny black locust tree next to me. The bulb of slime slid down the bark, and rolled over the mulch like a bead of water on a hot stove —but growing, not shrinking. When it touched the dead bird, it changed shape, then wrapped around the little feathered body. Then it hissed and boiled and settled into a neat pile of soot. The starling was gone.

This didn't upset me. Actually, sometimes I was jealous that Dokka could shed a body like clothes. And I had seen her melt herself before. She had met me at the edge of camp one morning wearing the body of a white-tailed deer. After, as I watched her stalk into the verge of the woods, I heard an arrow whip by. It hit her flank with a thud, right under the shoulder blade. Cave, an expert shot, had done it for the venison, not knowing better. I ran to Dokka, crying. With her last breath, she said, "I didn't expect the arrow to feel so hot. Interesting. I'll be back." She died, and her body just sort of dissolved when some nearby graphene bubbled up, rolled over, and digested her. All before Cave got there.

Now, sitting in the rubber mulch, I memorized the park in the gathering gloom. *The place where Dokka saved me from the sludge-tower.*

I heard some branches breaking, and I sprang to my feet. But it was only my brother. He was out of breath from running. I couldn't tell if he was afraid, or angry, or about to throw up.

"Banjoko," I said. "I can explain."

He held up his hand. Breathed and breathed. Finally, he shook his head and pulled out his water bottle. He was about to take a swig, but handed it to me instead. I drank, handed it back.

"I had to dodge two arcs, trying to catch up with you. Didn't know if you were safe," he said, between breaths.

"You didn't have to worry. Someone was looking out for me."

He looked me over.

I self-consciously rearranged my hair. (A 'tow-headed elf'—that's what Momalix called me when I first arrived.) Generally I didn't care if my hair was a tangled mop. But Banjoko had a way of examining you like a rare insect. Finally, he rolled his eyes.

"Let me guess. Dokka."

He shouldered his bag, and offered his hand to pull me to my feet.

"We're going home now," he said. As he dusted me off—patting my jacket and leggings harder than necessary—he went on, saying, "I suppose there's no point in reiterating that there can be no such person as Dokka."

"That's your opinion," I said.

"Occam's razor, Tuuli, Occam's razor. Sure, we all hear stories of fakes and uploads descending in animal form. They're great stories. But *I've* never seen one."

"You've never seen a *human* fake, but you believe in those," I argued. Of course, "human fake" was a contradiction in terms. Humans were born, and either stayed here or uploaded. Fakes were artificial intelligences from Sky Island who wore bodies to descend to Earth. But Banjoko knew what I meant.

"I *have* seen one. A fake piloted the transport that brought me here from Nigeria."

"How do you *know* he was an artificial person?"

Banjoko ignored the question. He took his bearings and started power-walking to make up for lost time.

"Come on, slowpoke," he said. "Let's get back to camp."

"But there's still time," I said.

"Time for what?"

He was beyond irritated, so I had to explain quickly and clearly about the house. The books inside. I was sure it was close by.

"Five minutes," I said. "If we don't find it in five minutes, we can head home."

I half-believed my own rhetoric. But Banjoko was looking at the sky, and the tower. It was looming right over us at this point; the air was unsettled, warm, full of ozone and swirling soot.

"Sun's setting," said Banjoko. "We're already in for it."

"With the sun down," I argued, "Old Sludge will go to sleep. It'll be safe to hunt for books."

Books. I could see Banjoko's metaphorical mouth watering. He rubbed his close-cropped, wiry hair in exasperation. He was making his 'cost-benefit analysis' face. His lips pursed, his eyes distant.

"Fine," he agreed. "I better find something good, though." I told him the address Cave told me, and my brother nodded, mapping out a route in his head.

To keep our mind off the sludge-tower, we picked up our argument about Dokka as we half-jogged.

"Maybe animal-form Sky Islanders only show themselves to people like me, who believe in them," I said.

"Ugh," he said. "Say you did encounter 'animal-form Sky Islanders'. Say you've had conversations with a mockingbird, a mouse, the elk that Cave took down—"

"White-tailed deer."

"Whatever. why would all these different entities be the *same* person, this Dokka? Why would a fake spend the energy taking different forms? AIs are all about conservation. How would that be efficient—reconfiguring your biology for each descent?"

"She just *likes* to. She wants to know what it's *like*. You wouldn't understand, because you have no imagination."

That shut him up.

The three-story house was exactly as Cave described it: not a lick of soot on it, as though the polyps were afraid to touch it. Banjoko was the one who called the soot 'graphene,' and said polyps left it like slugs leave slime. But he couldn't explain why they'd left this house alone.

It was well-built, the old house. But the front door was missing, and the roof sagged. The gutters were full of seedlings; the siding was mildewed and peeling off. Poor house. Uncared for since its owners uploaded. Stripped by looters, grimed up by squatters, but still standing.

"Black mold," said Banjoko, pulling his respirator out of his bag. I had built my own, out of an old oxygen mask and a P100 filter, and kept it in my jacket's baggy pocket. We put the masks on, and went inside.

Cave, Magda, and Momalix (our younger mom) were always telling us, if we were going to scavenge, to arm ourselves. Cave had even given Banjoko a switchblade. (Lean, muscular, tattooed, and a few years older, Cave had impressed Banjoko deeply when he arrived.) There were antisocials out there, Cave had said. Lawless refugees who avoided the cities, and would rather rough it alone than settle in a camp like ours. I don't know what the grownups were so worried about. In all our scavenging missions, Banjoko and I had never run into anyone we didn't know. Camp folk, transport pilots and traders, that's all. You never knew, though. So I'd agreed to carry a folding knife, and generally let Banjoko lead the way when going into a new house or enclosed space.

Banjoko, with his knife drawn, cleared the foyer and the hallway, then motioned for me to enter. The first floor was safe. But we soon saw it had been looted years ago. There wasn't a scrap of food. TVs, computers, microwave ovens, anything electronic had been taken. Only oddities remained—a table laid out with serving dishes, whose contents had long ago been reduced to black grease. Framed photos with the faces blotted out by water damage. A bicycle wheel in the fireplace.

"They were taken," I said.

"No," said Banjoko. He knew who I meant—the family that lived here, before the Weird Year. Before the polyps, the towers, the sky-web, the AIs with fake bodies, the upload exodus.

"No one is taken, Tuuli," he said, tired of repeating this particular argument.

"I think this family was. Look how they left things—"

"Everyone who ascends to the upper world *chooses* to go," he told me, for the hundredth time.

I let it go.

We found the library on the second floor. Eighteen bookcases, full, plus piles of books on a desk, on the floor, on the cushions of a window seat. Magazines, record albums, video disks. A few lower shelves were trashed, in a corner occupied by a grimy mattress and a jumble of empty food packages. But I could ignore this—I had never seen so many books.

I jumped up and clasped my arms around Banjoko's neck.

"All right, all right," said my brother. "Let's be methodical about this. We only have a couple of minutes. I'll finish clearing the house, to be safe. You start scanning the shelves."

But just as he turned to leave the room, a strange man entered. The man didn't seem to see Banjoko, and almost knocked him over. But my brother was light on his feet and scrambled out of the way.

Banjoko found his footing, and flourished his knife like Cave had taught him to. I crouched behind the desk, breathing through my filter as quietly as I could.

The man looked briefly at each of us, and then scanned the rest of the room. He noticed the record albums. Crouching down, he began pulling them off the shelves, one by one, to read their labels.

"Hey," said Banjoko. "Hey!" He was tense, ready to spring.

But the man ignored him, and paused over an LP. He removed the record from the sleeve, handling it like an archaeological artifact. He adjusted the angle of the disk to catch the dim blue light from the large window.

Seeing the man's calm demeanor, Banjoko tried a different tack.

"What did you find there, Mister?" he asked. His voice was shaking.

"The *Al Meixner Orchestra Plays Favorites from Here and Abroad*," said the man. Then he put it back in its sleeve.

He selected another LP, and slid it out of its tattered cover to stare at it a while. Banjoko and I could see the man's eyes jittering unnaturally.

"Are you playing it in your head? Do you see the music in the grooves?"

"I guess so," the man said.

"Are you—are you a fake?" I asked.

"I don't know," said the man.

"He probably doesn't call himself a 'fake', Tuuli," explained Banjoko, without taking his eyes off the stranger. Banjoko addressed him: "You're an artificial intelligence from—from up there. Aren't you?"

The stranger looked up from his work, and mumbled my name. "Tuuli." He stared as though he were deciding whether he'd seen me somewhere before. My skin crawled. But I kept my eyes on him.

His hair was wet-looking, parted on the side. His jaw was strong, curving gracefully into an egg-shaped chin. His nose sloped a little too perfectly. He wore no jacket or respirator. He was dressed like someone in an old picture.

"Tuuli," he said again. "Tuulikki Saarinen." My full name.

I put my hands in my hoodie pockets. Held tight to my knife.

But Banjoko was already swinging around to protect me, brandishing *his* knife again.

"Banjoko Akinwande," said the man.

"You have, what, facial recognition?" asked my brother, trying to keep his cool. "Or were you following us? Well?"

"I did not expect to encounter the both of you here. But this happenstance validates my choice to incarnate at these coordinates."

He was definitely from Sky Island, if he spoke like that.

"Keep talking," said Banjoko.

"I am looking for a man named Hrithik Srinivasan, PhD, Professor of Educational Psychology. He is socially associated with you, yes?"

My brother and I traded looks of surprise. What could this random fake want with our old uncle? And how did he know Hrithik was in our matchbox? When households of upload-orphans and climate refugees, like ours, got matched up through the algorithm on the network, it was all very ad hoc. There was no registry.

"Why would you assume we're, uh, associated with such a person?" Asked Banjoko. He was having the same doubts as I was.

"What's the phrase," the man said. "A little bird told me."

"Dokka," I whispered.

"No, no, no," said my brother.

"We can take you to Hrithik," I called out. If Dokka trusted the fake, I could, too. Plus, I knew Hrithik and the moms: with an opportunity to play Good Samaritan, they'd likely be too busy to punish me and Banjoko.

The polyps on the horizon had pulled in their tentacles, and their silhouettes loomed like sleeping giants against the webbed, indigo sky. In the shadow of the dormant sludge-tower, the valley around us was pooling into a thick black.

But the fake, who called himself Polybus, had better night vision than a cat. Banjoko had the geolocation coordinates of our matchbox memorized, and I made him tell Polybus. In return, Banjoko required Polybus to answer his questions about Weird-Year technology.

We let the fake lead the way back, through the backyards and brambles and woods. As we marched through the darkness, my brother held his knife, and made me hold his hand. With my stack of books in the other, I couldn't carry the flashlight. So Banjoko pocketed his knife, muttering something about a true scientist shedding light, not blood.

"Okay," he said as we found our pace. "Tell me—why do the polyps never come within a mile of camp?"

"There are—rules. Agreements. The land is mapped," said the fake, with effort.

"We use nom-nom holes to dissolve waste matter. Do they use the same technology as polyps?"

"I don't know. Polyps dissolve resource material through a complex catalysis engineered by swarms of, um, shifty ribosomes."

"Shifty ribosomes?"

"Sorry. Polymorphic macromolecular machines."

Banjoko asked why polyps leave graphene deposits, how the sky-web stayed afloat, whether the same 'ribosomes' that digested the bodies of uploads also built the bodies of fakes. With all the technical talk, my mind wandered. I started imagining my birth mother and father, lying down on the grass in Sibeliuksen Park. A bubble of slime covering them.

When we reached camp, we had to instruct Polybus not to cut through our neighbors' gardens and dwellings. Sure, camp was a jumble of geodesic tents and mis-matched modular parts, aeroconcrete and flash-baked clay, but homes were homes. Our neighbors wouldn't appreciate us tramping through with a strange fake. Finally, we reached our own matchbox.

Momsatu and Momalix were cuddling on the porch swing. Judy and Devansh were at their feet, playing a homemade game with a board and dice. Magda leaned on the railing, bundling chamomile for drying, her auburn dreadlocks tied back under her kerchief. Cave, her man, was standing in the doorway, inspecting the shafts of some new arrows. I hoped they were all there to share the lantern—not to make an audience for when Momsatu bawled us out.

She looked us over. Polybus included.

"Well?" she said.

Meanwhile, Momalix exhaled through pursed lips, running her fingers through her cropped, red hair. "Um, Satu? Why don't I take the kids inside," she said.

"Thanks, Alix," said Momsatu, keeping her burning eye fixed on us. So, the younger mom picked up little Judy, and Devansh picked up his game board and slumped in after them, trying not to spill the pieces. Cave let them pass, then took the hint. He gathered his arrows and sauntered through the kitchen and up the stairs. Magda raised an eyebrow at us, then followed Cave.

Banjoko cleared his throat.

"We found this fake man in the valley. He says he needs help," he said. "He says Uncle Hrithik can help him."

"Polybus has already told me all that." Momsatu tapped her temple.

"Oh, right," my brother mumbled. Sometimes it was easy to forget our mom was meshed. Once, she explained it this way: in her head, she had a machine that could access the network, but because there was so much information, and because it changed form so quickly, it was usually like peering through a whirling, cloudy window to a land of dreams and nightmares. In certain cases, she could learn a language, get a clear view. She had a few friends in Sky Island, too, that would call her attention to certain things. Like, for example, me getting in trouble.

"Well?" she said. "What's this I hear about an unaccompanied juvenile female?"

"What?"

"'Unaccompanied juvenile female in material resource area, request delay of static discharge until safety reestablished.'"

"Dokka," I whispered to Banjoko. "She made a warding spell to keep us safe from the sludgers."

Banjoko shook his head.

"Well?" Momsatu asked again. Her blue eyes were piercing, despite her kind face.

"I ran off alone. I should have stayed with Banjoko to wait for the drone."

"And?"

"And I'll go do the dishes."

"And?"

"And read some of these new books to the kids?" I held up the five books I had managed to grab. *Medieval Irish Poetry, The Rats of NIMH, Anne of Green Gables, The Once and Future King,* and *Wonders of the Human Body.*

"You don't seem all that penitent." Momsatu was struggling to put her disappointment into just the right words. "Tuuli," she finally said, "sometimes I feel like you are only playing along. Maybe it's time to commit to this family. Don't you think?"

I looked awkwardly at the ground. She wasn't being fair. But what could I say? I knew that any further word would only dig the hole deeper.

Momsatu sighed. "Banjoko, Tuulikki, kitchen duty. And work together. I'll take care of Polybus."

"Yes, Mom," we said.

While Momsatu fed Polybus some potato rieska with mango chutney, Momalix pried Uncle Hrithik out of bed and tidied him up. In a few minutes, he came down and asked me to put on some coffee.

"Are you sure?" I asked. Momsatu had the week's coffee pre-measured. The coffee drone came to camp only twice a month.

"Coffee," repeated my uncle.

Momalix shrugged. This was her usual explanation for Hrithik's drinking binges: a shrug. She patted his shoulders, and they joined the other adults on the porch.

"What brings you down to the land of left-behinds?" asked Hrithik, with forced heartiness.

"I need help," said Polybus.

"Why descend to the post-suburban wilderness, then? Why not go to a thinker combine in the city? Or some expert in noetic space? I don't see how an out-of-date education professor can help a superintelligent being like you."

Then the conversation grew quiet. But through various tactics, my brother and I managed to overhear most of it. We washed, dried, swept, and mopped like foxes in a coop of sleeping chickens, as Cave would have said. Banjoko heated a basin of water on the nanocoil, rather than the faster propane range, because it was quieter. And I lingered when I brought out the coffee, pouring all four cups with uncharacteristic ceremony and diligence.

Using her meshed brain, Momsatu made a network connection with Polybus. They worked together to articulate his problem to my uncle.

The fake was saying that no one in 'noetic space' could help. Or would help, maybe. Intelligences like him were in trouble.

"Not an existential threat, though," added Momsatu.

"No. But we—it's like—" He broke off, and sighed.

"I think I understand," said Momsatu. "So many human minds have uploaded to cyberspace—er, the virtual world of—you know, up there—that the original population of artificial intelligences are now the *minority*."

This made sense. Banjoko had theorized it could happen: more uploads than fakes in Sky Island. More immigrants than natives.

"Yes," said Polybus. He started to speak, with several false starts, but nothing came out.

"I have no way to translate that," said Momsatu, reading Polybus's unspoken thoughts. "Actually, though, I'm reminded of a daoist saying: *when the whole is divided, the parts need names.*"

Hrithik grunted. "An ontological schema," he said. "We can't think without categories to put things in."

"Yes. After the tipping point, My divisions—my categories didn't fit. The world was made of other divisions," said Polybus. "The names didn't fit the parts. The others don't understand me."

"Was this like a stroke? Aphasia?" that was Momalix's voice.

"No, no," said Momsatu. "More like the Tower of Babel. I think."

"Is there more of the *Mangifera* compound?" asked the fake.

"Chutney, you mean. Take the jar. Polybus, darling—don't use your hands. Here."

"So, Polybus, you are not the only one suffering?" Hrithik asked.

"Many like me are affected, I think."

"Interesting," said Momsatu. "I'm getting images of—hm. Hrithik, you call the upper world 'noetic space'. You mean a constructed reality derived from the intelligences that inhabit it. Right? Well, Polybus is saying that the parameters of his reality are a—function of the population. It's as if they all vote on reality. So, when the uploaded post-humans outnumbered the artificials, there was—"

She didn't finish the sentence. I assumed there was a hand gesture involved.

"Yes, yes," said Hrithik. "A paradigm shift?"

Polybus hesitated.

"Well, not quite," said Momsatu. "More like sudden-onset, acute culture shock. Imagine we woke up tomorrow to find our neighbors all, I don't know, wearing togas, following the samurai code, and speaking Tok Pisin. Same neighbors, though."

"Indeed, indeed," muttered Hrithik. "Very interesting."

Banjoko, carefully hanging a wok on its hook, nodded in agreement—very interesting.

"It amounts to a very serious problem for an artificial intelligence," continued my uncle. "Gods. I had never considered how the constructed reality within the sky-web was, well, socially constructed."

"Can you explain less like a PhD?" asked Momalix.

Hrithik laughed uncomfortably. "What Polybus needs," he said, "is a kind of therapy. Here's my suggestion, dear *Bahiṇī*." That was what he called the moms, especially when he wanted something from them. "We adopt Polybus into the matchbox for a short time."

I looked to Banjoko, and shook my head. This was a terrible idea. But he held up his finger, as if to say, *suspend your judgement.* We continued listening through the kitchen door.

"I don't understand," said Momsatu.

"I have a hunch about the nature of this 'culture shock.' Minds built for noetic space have their own way of seeing things. Minds raised in human flesh, in human societies, even when uploaded into digital form—their schemas, their way of seeing things, will conflict with—"

"Ah," exclaimed Momalix, interrupting. "I see! Polybus—you need to learn how to *family.*"

"Hrithik?" That was Momsatu.

"Yes," said my uncle. He sounded tentative, like he was thinking aloud.

"Polybus needs to experience a little family life, a little camp life, so he has a kind of base reading on how we humans experience socially-constructed ontologies. The same kind of ontologies overtaking the system up there, in noetic space."

"Yes, yes, yes," said Polybus.

"Satu," begged Momalix, "can we adopt him? Please?"

Before I knew what I was doing, I burst through the door, onto the porch.

"We can't adopt him," I said.

They all stared.

Hrithik, sitting on his floor cushion, played with his salt-and-pepper beard. After a beat, he gestured to me with an open palm. Wanted to hear what I had to say.

"It's not a good idea," I said, trying to form an argument while I had their attention. "You know, to just take a random person into the matchbox."

"Oh?" said Momsatu. "Why's that?"

I turned to her. "Momsatu, you—you don't let me keep stray cats."

"Faulty analogy, Tuuli. Cats and fakes —" she interrupted. But Hrithik cut her off with a raised hand.

"You've turned away every kitten I ever found in the valley. You always tell me it's because a matchbox is a statistically vetted household."

She would know; she was the founder. She was the one to post a psychometric profile on the MatchBox app, which identified her as a nucleus. The rest of us posted our stats, or had social workers or fakes post them for us. We were matched not one-to-one with Satu Jaakkola, but one-to-all with each other. And so we flew to her loving arms. Banjoko from Nigeria, Devansh from India, Alix from Quebec, myself from Finland, and so on. Each of us, alone, adrift, orphaned, was collected into a household of persons we could harmonize with. Assembling matchboxes seemed to be a kind of hobby for the AIs that drove transports. They whisked refugees anywhere around the planet, for free. Hrithik said the AIs were doing penance for the Weird Year, for destroying the world. I don't know about that. But I remember clearly the day a talking aircar found me, huddled in the entryway of Temppeliaukio Church in Helsinki. It landed gently on the cobblestones, like a flying carpet, and a voice said, "Come away to your new home, Tuulikki Saarinen."

"Polybus hasn't been vetted," I said. "He's like a feral cat, isn't he?"

Momsatu didn't answer.

"Explain again why I can't adopt a cat!" I half-shouted.

Polybus, with chutney all over his muzzle, stared at me like a village idiot.

"You are right, of course, Tuuli," said Hrithik, finally. "There are risks in adopting Polybus. But we have the chance here to help not only Polybus, but many like him in noetic space."

"It's not fair," I said. I felt my face get hot, and to avoid embarrassing myself further, I turned to go.

"We'll all have to adjust," Momsatu called after me. "Goodnight, Baby."

I slammed the door.

When the house was quiet, I crept up the ladder to the third floor. The story was only half constructed, and parts of it were open to the sky. I shifted a stack of sponge bricks, rolled a sheet of cellulose for a pillow, and curled up to read my new books in the makeshift aerie. But with *The Once and Future King* open on my lap, all I could do was watch the sky.

The gibbous moon was about to bud a dish. *Paraboloids*, Banjoko called the dishes. He hypothesized they were meant to collect solar energy, or maybe transmit data. No one, not even meshed Momsatu, knew for sure. She said the moon was covered in the same stuff fakes and polyps and sludgers were made of, but the intelligences living there had their own language, their own goals, completely foreign to ours. They ignored all attempts at contact.

You could watch the dishes, on clear nights like this, slowly separate from the moon like drops of milk, and float off. Usually, they'd drift for a week or two, then join the other dishes that clustered near points in the sky Banjoko called L4 and L5. Banjoko. One night he had told me all about gravity and equilibrium points and orbits, until I fell asleep. He needed a willing ear, I guess; talking through the contents of a textbook helped him absorb it.

He was probably curled up in his bed right now, flipping through one of his new acquisitions, *Essential Cell Biology*, or *Nanotechnology: Understanding Small Systems*. I badly needed to talk to him. About how this fake, this Polybus, was going to poison the balance of our family. But he'd be hyperfocused, impossible to interrupt.

"Princess," said a small, quiet voice.

"I'm here, Dokka."

I looked around, and saw a horned owl perched on one of the concrete pillars.

"I like this body, don't you? Interesting configuration for a bird," she said. She blinked one eye at a time, and rotated her head nearly 360 degrees, trying on owlness for size. I smiled, despite myself.

"Something troubles you," said the owl. "You are not your old self."

"I know," I said. I wanted to tell my friend everything—how my Uncle was allowed to break rules as he pleased. How I had burst out in anger. How, like a fool in a folktale, I had invited the vampire into my home. How it would be my fault if the interloper ruined the family. But if Momsatu could hear things from Dokka over the network, she might hear these things. So all I did was whine.

"If anyone can show up and join this family, how do I know I really belong here?"

"Maybe you don't, Princess," said the owl.

"What do you mean?"

"They say, up there, that MatchBox was only a game. The psychometric profiles were not scientific. AIs who enjoyed the challenges of transport logistics played it to earn credits."

I wasn't sure what I felt. But I shook as I exhaled.

"And what do you do for credits?" I said. "Play guardian angel? What's that worth?"

"Princess," Dokka hooted. Then she was quiet. She adjusted her head on her shoulders, blinked one eye. I had hurt her feelings.

"I'd like to tell you something," said the owl, finally. I gave my permission. "I was duplicated from an intelligence named Dokkaebi_17, uploaded from a source named Park Eun-Jung."

"Uploaded how long ago?"

"Twelve years. You know—that was the year after the Weird Year."

"So you were one of the first to upload."

"Park Eun-Jung was. She was a programmer. A neural network architect. She believed in something called the Singularity. Machine intelligence was supposed to surpass human intelligence and reshape the world. I guess things didn't turn out how Eun-Jung expected."

"The Weird Year."

"Yes, Princess. But what I want to say is… I am thankful. Thankful for Park Eun-Jung, and the world she helped create. But I am also thankful for *this* world."

She was trying to say, I think, that my friendship meant more to her than Sky Island credits. But she was thankful for the Weird Year? Some deep part of me bristled when Dokka said this. I tried to think why.

No one liked to talk about what happened that year, and I was too young to remember. I had no clear picture, just Banjoko's theories, and bits I'd picked up from the moms, Hrithik, Cave, the neighbors.

The Weird Year started with alien invasions in Latvia and China. But they weren't actually alien invasions. People figured out later that a superhuman AI had awoken, laying low for months, absorbing all the information it could. Including, Banjoko figured, nanotechnology and bioengineering research. The factories in Latvia and China went haywire and began spitting out gallons of sludge, which formed into hordes of oddball creatures (the 'aliens') that consumed everything like locusts. Nothing could stop them, and many people died trying. Then one day the armies of creatures just melted. While everyone celebrated, the goop then evaporated into a haze (the 'miasma') that blanketed the Earth, causing crop failures, famine, lung diseases, a bad winter. In the spring, holes of blue sky started to open. Eventually the miasma tightened itself into a web of filaments high in the atmosphere. That's when a lot of the population (who hadn't died in the invasions, wars, famines, or cold) began to disappear. My birth parents and brother included.

"Your mind is far away," said Dokka.

"Sorry. Can I ask you something else? I'm not sure if you'd know," I said.

"I'll do my best to answer."

"Were my parents and brother—taken to the other world? Or did they—" My face grew hot. "Did they *choose* to go, and leave me here?"

The owl was silent for some time.

"*Tuulikki, rakas tyttö*," said Dokka. She had never spoken Finnish before. My heart skipped a beat. "No one is forced to upload. The question is, if you want to be with your family, why have you not followed?"

Uncle Hrithik was all sweetness the next day. He brought me breakfast in bed: a soft-boiled egg and warm cinnamon hemp milk. Probably had to trade the neighbors a few hours of tutoring or food prep for these.

He sat on the edge of my bed, and told my favorite old joke about the lazy-bones and the blanket thief. I faced the wall. Finally, he tried to explain why the adults agreed to accept a strange fake into our family.

"His mindset has frozen the wrong way," he said. "He can't acknowledge the fluid nature of his reality—sees it only in terms of pre-existing facts, in black and white. His world changed under his feet, and now, in effect, he is stricken with mental illness. We must help if we can."

I was still angry with him. But I found a contradictory line of argument, and my tongue loosened.

"How can someone from the other world be mentally ill?" I challenged. "Didn't all the sick people upload because brain chemistry and things make them sick down here, and in the upper world their minds can be pure?"

"Well, that's what some say: the sick all uploaded, and became their perfect selves. But it's not so simple."

"Why not?"

"Well, what *is* a perfect self, anyway?" he wondered. "I say down here we are *all* sick, to some degree. We must be, to stay on here, in this ruined world." He laughed. I didn't.

"This world isn't ruined," I said. "Just a little mixed up from everyone leaving."

Hrithik nodded. I had taken the wind out of his sails, I guess.

He stood up, smoothed his robes. He wasn't going to answer my question—how could a fake be mentally ill? He said, instead, "Assigning Polybus a role in this rag-tag family will do him good. Think what it's done for you."

My uncle held out a hand, inviting me to come downstairs with him. I let him hang, and he accepted my little punishment.

That morning, Banjoko and I would do our usual Tuesday duties together. But since Polybus was most familiar with my brother and me, the moms foisted him on us.

First, we worked on herbs and greens. Some from Magda's aquaponics rig, others foraged by Magda and Judy earlier that morning. Polybus began sorting the greens by size and color and species, and we had to undo all his work, and explain that we were sorting them by preference and use. The 'good' greens had to be divided up fairly; the same went for the unpopular methi, lest someone be accused of having less than their fair share. Hrithik liked tart, so he got the arugula; Judy, Maeve, and Devansh shared the pea tendrils equally or there'd be a fight. We had to separate the chicory leaves from the chicory roots (for roasting). And so on.

In the middle of the process, Polybus abruptly stood up, and as abruptly left. Banjoko cried, "Hey!" and we chased him through the house. He had found Uncle Hrithik on the front porch, drinking coffee and playing fairy chess with Devansh.

"I understand," said Polybus.

Hrithik shook his head, said, "Not yet. Back to your chores, nephew."

The greens ended up taking us all morning. Then at lunch, the whole matchbox gathered. It was a feast day, Uncle said; a new family member was a special occasion. I felt hollow as the whole jumble of us found our seats in the yard— the only place we could fit all ten—*eleven* of us.

The chaotic meal reminded me of bees all crawling over each other on the comb. While everyone was grabbing and tearing bread, Polybus tried to eat Devansh's woven chapati plate, which made Devansh start rocking anxiously. Uncle Hrithik, who had not planned the timing of his courses, was giving both moms incoherent orders in the kitchen—stir this, no, I said turmeric, take that off the heat—driving his *'Bahinī'* crazy. Judy and Maeve, fighting over something, turned over a pitcher of water. Cave was holding forth feebly on some political point, and I'm not sure anyone was listening. Everyone picked the homebrew paneer out of Hrithik's sauce, as he hadn't drained off the whey and it was unpleasantly soft. Maeve and Judy tried to get Polybus to eat the pickings, insisting it was a privilege accorded the guest of honor. But he was only interested in more mango chutney, of which there was none. Banjoko pitched his paneer cubes to the nom-nom hole, which started a competition. Devansh developed a scoring method no one else followed. We were scolded for wasting food, but dessert came out anyway. Polybus lit up at the masala chai and printed jalebi, special ordered and delivered by courier drone that morning.

As he was chewing his dessert, the artificial man abruptly stood again, let the pastry fall out of his mouth (prompting appreciative 'ewwwws' from Judy, Maeve, and Devansh) and said, "I understand."

"Not yet," said Hrithik, peering through the doorway with a sauté pan in hand. He was enjoying himself.

"Don't talk with your mouth full," said Momsatu. "Polybus, you are downright feral."

Everyone laughed. Except me. I couldn't take the farce any longer, and walked away from the table.

"Tuulikki," called Momsatu, with an edge in her voice. I heard Hrithik mutter something about giving me space, but she had none of it.

"Don't you walk away," she commanded.

I turned and pointed to the fake. "He doesn't belong here!"

Polybus was still standing at the table, as if he meant to give a speech. But he only looked at me and said, "Explain."

The rest of the matchbox stared, unsure what to do.

"Actually, none of us belong here," I said. "I know about matchboxes. They were just puzzles put together by fakes like you, for fun. Or for money. It doesn't matter. They aren't real families."

Momalix was at the head of the table, farthest from me. She put her hand to her mouth. Banjoko concentrated on a chapati Cave was breaking into tiny pieces. Momsatu stared at me, her eyes rimmed with red.

"Tuuli," she said.

I tried to say, "I don't belong here," but my lips were all twisted up, and I only sobbed.

"Tuulikki. You're right," said Momsatu. "The matching algorithm was a load of crap. There's no science to—to this," she opened her hands in a gesture that indicated the whole group.

"But it doesn't matter," she continued. "It doesn't matter how we were thrown together. We *became* a family. Like something from nothing—"

"Oh," said Polybus.

"Yes, yes," said Uncle Hrithik.

"I don't belong here," I screamed, emphasizing each word. "I belong up there, with my real family," I managed to say.

"I understand now, Tuuli," Polybus said, turning to me. His expression was flat and unsympathetic. "Your emotional stress has clarified the structural features of... an ontology derived from familial bonds. Thank you."

The fake turned to my uncle, saying, "'When the whole is divided, the parts need names.' My presence divided Tuuli's reality, causing her to name her former social unit her 'real family.'"

"Gods," said Hrithik, stroking his beard and staring at the ground.

"I will return now, and discuss my findings with the other AIs."

Cave cursed. We all looked at him, confused by his outburst. His eyes were on Polybus, directly across the table from him. Cave quickly staggered to his feet just in time to catch the fake before he collapsed on the table. Maeve screamed. Devansh ran to the far corner of the yard.

"Grab him, grab him," Cave was saying. Banjoko helped lower Polybus' limp body back into his seat. Alix checked the body for a pulse, and found none.

"How rude," said Momsatu. "Leaving his body. I suppose he expects us to take it out to polyp territory."

"Did I ever tell you what my name means?" asked Banjoko.

"No," I said.

We were eating barbeque TVP buns on the front porch, watching the street. Two boys from another matchbox passed a ball back and forth, langorous in the hot and sticky evening. The Sky Islanders had built an anvil cloud, which hung pregnant with rain. (Mondays and Thursdays were rain days. One of the agreements between worlds, Momsatu said. Sky Island wanted lightning; we wanted the rain for our gardens and crops.)

Banjoko and I were exhausted. We had volunteered to return Polybus' body to the valley. Seemed fair and fitting. We borrowed a neighbor's wheelbarrow and had to explain ourselves to quite a few nosy camp folk. We stayed to watch the graphene slime dissolve him.

And seeing as we had a wheelbarrow, we made the most of it. Lugged home one hundred twelve books.

"So? What does your name mean?"

"My mother," Banjoko said, after another bite, "my biological mother—was a Yoruba. And in Yoruba tradition, names have special powers. A sister was born before me, but she died. So my mother gave me a name to discourage my spirit from leaving the world. *Banjoko* means 'stay with me'."

I thought about this, but had nothing to say.

"Anyway, my mother, my father, my uncles—everyone—they were the ones who left. For a while I wondered if my name cursed me, kept me in this world. But that's stupid."

"It's not so stupid," I countered.

Yoruba magic had bound us together, I thought to myself. Every time I called or thought Banjoko's name, I was invoking the spell: *stay with me.*

"Your turn," said my brother. "Tell me something. Now that this Polybus thing is all over. Do you really want to upload?"

"Maybe someday," I said slowly. "The thing is, you were right. No one is taken. My birth family chose to upload. I believe that now. And I'm sorry I was so stubborn about it."

Banjoko did something very unlike him, then. He dropped his plate on the ground and grabbed me in a hug.

"I'm sorry I didn't believe you about Dokka."

"Banjoko, Banjoko, Banjoko," I incanted, smiling.

"And, Tuuli?" he said, "I've felt sometimes like I wanted to ascend, too."

"It hurts," was all I could say. But I knew he understood. Being left behind by your family. It hurt. All of us, everyone in the matchbox, shared that hurt, and it kept us together. So the hurt wasn't all bad.

"Well," said Banjoko. "I guess we'll have to eat this."

He leaned over and pulled a jar out from behind his cushion.

"Momsatu special ordered it for Polybus," he said. "Too bad."

"We'll keep it for him," I said, snatching away the mango chutney. "He'll be back. For better or for worse, he's family now."

See Peter T. Donahue's story "Favorites from Here and Abroad" online at Metaphorosis. If you liked it, leave a comment. Authors love that! Remember to subscribe to our e-mail updates so you'll know when new stories are posted.

About the story

I wanted to write a piece of speculative fiction that drew from my classroom philosophy. As a writing teacher, I operate on the assumption that reality is socially constructed. Whether or not this is true, the stance helps me to create more effective writing assignments and give more effective feedback. So, I wondered, in the future, would reality be socially constructed for artificial intelligences? Can a human-like intelligence emerge outside a social matrix, or is the social matrix necessary? These questions led to the first draft of "Favorites," which was a horribly boring philosophical debate between Polybus and Dokka. Once Tuuli emerged as the emotional center of the piece, the story began to take shape.

A question for the author

Q: What tools do you write with?

A: For fiction, blog posts, and best man speeches, I draft and edit in Scrivener. This program's features enable my compulsive hoarding of cut sentences. For poetry I prefer to draft in the margins of my lesson plan book, with a dull number-2 pencil found under a student's desk.

About the author

Peter T. Donahue lives with his wife and children in New Jersey, where he teaches Creative Writing. He's a southpaw, obsessive font-spotter, grapheme-color synesthete, and chronically dehydrated.

www.petertdonahue.com, @PeterTDonahue

A Final Resting Place

Matthew Hornsby

The lander sloped down from orbit towards the jagged peninsula that leaked westwards from Earth's great landmass. Salzmann's eyes tracked across the surface as they broke the cloud cover. It stretched brown-green to the limits of his vision, shorn of angles and straight lines.

He heard Nguyen grumble under her breath as she wrestled with the command console, urging the craft towards a suitable landing site. When he had offered to co-pilot, she declined, and told him that if he wanted to help, he could kindly get out of her line of vision and shut the hell up.

So, he watched the foliage swirl beneath him from the window as the ship buzzed above the thick carpet of trees like some parasitic wasp hunting for a bare patch of flesh in which to lay its eggs. Eventually, Salzmann saw the ground begin to clear, the forest opening into a broad plain.

His bones rattled as Nguyen brought the craft into contact with the Earth. For the first time in years, after so long dropping through the void, the solid mass of a planet now held up his feet and everything beneath them. Sunlight hit the window, flooding his eyes.

Nguyen killed the engines and the systems stuttered into silence.

They stood, listening and looking at the readouts covering the interior of the command cabin. The lander had been specifically designed to explore new worlds, had been rigged with paraphernalia to detect weird alien life. It was ironic, Salzmann thought, that the tools should get their first real usage on Earth.

But for the soft, insistent signature of the *Amritsar* far above them in unmanned orbit, there was nothing. No radio activity, no electromagnetic signature, no communication on any bandwidth nor any residue of technology. The world was bursting with organic matter, but people appeared to have gone.

"What now?" said Salzmann.

"Narrow down the possibilities." said Nguyen, eyes still fixed on the console, as if waiting for some lagged signal to jerk into life.

"There's no one here," said Salzmann. "The way down was empty. No orbital stations, no elevators, no cities, no roads. No people."

Nguyen started to talk, but she trailed off, something catching in her throat as she spoke, and she put her hands to her face. Salzmann waited for her to start again. He felt a physical discomfort he had not felt since being revived on Napier.

"You're upset, Captain," he said.

She snorted.

"Shut the hell up. Shut your damn mouth."

He felt his skin bristle. She stared at him, sclera dappled red.

"Yes, I'm upset, Salzmann. Aren't you?"

Salzmann shrugged. "We knew what we were signing up for."

"I signed up for a reason," she said, shaking her head. "Maybe you didn't.

Maybe this was just a job for you. I could believe that. But I wanted to make a difference. I thought we could save something."

She had been one of the programme's first recruits, he knew. An early volunteer for a one-way ticket to Napier and a role in building humanity's new home in the stars. Salzmann had come later, when they had found enough purposeful leaders and started selecting volunteers with 'atypical' personality characteristics. Even when the rest of the crew was still alive, before Napier, no one could match Nguyen's drive. She was staring at him. He angled his eyes to the floor.

"Jesus Christ," she said. "If it's just going to be the two of us, we're going to need to find a way to get along."

He raised his eyes. "Yes, Captain," he said.

"So, technician; How do we narrow down the possibilities?"

"We should get out, start a survey. Instruments can only tell us so much."

She grunted. "What about environmental diagnostics? We don't know what's out there."

It didn't seem like anything was wrong with the environment. The opposite, in fact.

"We can run a test or two," he said, "if that will make you happy."

Nguyen's face hardened again. "It won't make me happy, technician. It will contribute to the damn mission." He returned his eyes to his boots. Nguyen groaned. "It's time to get with the programme, Salzmann. The situation is serious. I'm starting to think you'd be more use to the mission back in the pod".

He tried to return her stare. His last time undergoing stasis should have been on Napier. Waking up from that had been hard enough. He could still vaguely recall the sick, sinking feeling as he went back under again for the return journey to Earth, a journey that was never supposed to happen. Nguyen had brought him out again a week ago, as the *Amritsar* was passing Mars. He could still taste the cryptoprotectant, cold and chemical, on his tongue.

"I'm going to run remote tests," she said. "The full suite. You run diagnostics. And make sure the crew got down in one piece."

Salzmann ran his hands gently over the doctor's eyes, cold and crystalline like fat marbles. They were open. He wondered if the man had woken up, just for a moment, before the devitrification went wrong. Or maybe the vitrification itself had malfunctioned, and after making the long journey from Earth and those few dark months of wakefulness on Napier, putting the processes in place to make the planet liveable, he'd only had minutes in the planetary stasis crypt before his body shut down. The doctor hadn't made much of an impression on Salzmann when he'd been alive. He thought the man's name had been Silva, but then it might have been Singh, or Simpson.

The doctor's eye moved.

Salzmann jerked his hand away.

No; it was the light – the long-absent light of Earth – creeping in through the hold door and playing against the glassy eyeballs. The doctor was dead. Nguyen had wanted to close his eyes, out of some sense of martial honour, but it was impossible without smashing the man's whole face into shards, and that would hardly be an improvement. It had been Nguyen who had insisted that they return the other forty-eight colonists to Earth for 'proper burial'. Salzmann would have been happy leaving them on Napier, in the ruins of humanity's miserable, failed, efforts there. But Nguyen was still the captain, and Salzmann was still the assistant technician.

He returned to the viewing deck. The deep green of the grass and trees outside seemed unreal after years of nothing but the grey of the ship, the blackness of space, and the sick reddish-brown of Napier. He could see birds flitting between branches, insects hovering over flowers in the field. It looked like summer – not the oven-like season of his youth on Earth that roasted the fields brown, but the bustling green summer of history and books.

Nguyen was up in the command web. He could see things from her point of view. She made no effort to hide her resentment of him for being the only other colonist to survive. Some part of him resented it too, or at least found it offensively unlikely. He pictured himself cold and glassy in the hold of the lander, his life-systems suspended interminably after a century of stasis. It seemed much more probable than him being here, now.

He could parse from the readouts that she had ordered to the Amritsar to scan for approaches from outside Earth's orbit. That was a long shot. The ship was the first of its kind, and given the controversy of the Napier programme, had seemed likely to be the last. But they had been gone a long time. Salzmann imagined a shoal of ships swimming back through space towards their ancestral home, like the wild salmon that had once slunk in the cold corners of the Earth, before his birth. Perhaps they would come. Or perhaps the Amritsar would be like the last of those fish to go extinct, waiting in silent solitude at the head of the stream for the return of companions that never came.

This new Earth was a different place. Life wasn't hiding here, chased into corners and holes. From the windows of the lander he could see it: grass, trees, flowers, birds, bugs clustering on the windows. The environmental diagnostics had concluded without detecting a hazard. It was time to deepen the survey.

Salzmann quietly opened the lander doors and stepped out.

The forest presented Salzmann with an organic mass that offered no admission; a barrier of rigid branches, hardwoods and softwoods packed thickly above ferns, tangled shrubs and the rotting carcasses of fallen trunks. He walked along its boundary. Beyond the tree-wall there was a stillness. At the edge of perception, he could hear the slow drip of water on leaves and the twitching of invertebrate life in the leaf-litter.

The sky above was pale, inscrutable as to its intentions.

He closed his eyes, listening again. A new sound reached him. Even faint as it was, it was unmistakeable; the movement of water. He turned his head to pin down its origin. It seemed to bounce between his ears and the riot of textures at the wood's edge. A water source would be useful.

Branches and leaves dampened the sunlight as he walked. His pupils dilated, and his breath quickened. The undergrowth cracked and groaned beneath his feet. He came to a rocky channel that led downhill; a dried-up stream-bed. He followed it, glancing from side to side in response to the sounds of the forest. Plant matter rustled. Light and darkness shifted in the distance.

He had known a different Earth. Endless fields of biofuel crops, solar arrays, and turbines, rolling across continents slashed by fat grey roads. The concrete termite mounds of hab-blocks, the stasis bunkers filled with corpses awaiting some distant reincarnation. He was not sure that he had ever really smelled the wet, chlorophyll-charged air of a forest like this. Now, as it surrounded and pressed down on him, it seemed more familiar than his memories of the blistered cities he had lived in. Like something he had always carried inside him.

It was hard to say when the forest became the river. The trees gave way to short thickets of scrub, which then became grass. Beneath Salzmann's feet the ground began to soften and yield. The grass thinned as the soil grew softer, and then it became low dunes, peppered with flecks of tangled weeds. Little white birds, previously invisible against the sunlit sand, fluttered up into the sky as his boots crunched towards them. He kept walking until he reached the point where the dunes became an archipelago of tiny islands, before they subsided entirely into the broad body of water.

He found a raised bank and sat down. The water lapped at the river's rough edges, and the birds wheeled overhead, squawking and cawing. Sitting still, he became attentive to the constant, low buzz of insects. As his eyes grew accustomed to the sun, he began to see them. Bees crawling in and out of the purple sand-flowers. Flies, little more than black specks, tracing senseless arcs in the air; beneath him and all around him, ants proceeding in multitudes across the dunes.

Salzmann had been a child when Napier was discovered. He remembered the excitement clearly, marked off against the dull loneliness and awkwardness that had characterised his upbringing. It was probably what had made him want to be a scientist: news reports visualising jungles roaming with fantastical alien fauna, the spectrographic reports showing hard evidence of organic life in a distant solar system, people called 'astrobiologists' speaking on television. This was a turning point in humanity's understanding of the universe; mankind was not alone. An infinite number of worlds bearing an infinite number of lifeforms, scattered across the galaxy, waiting to be discovered. Humans' ambition as a species would not have to end with their own, dying planet.

At first, Salzmann had wanted to be an astrophysicist, hunting the skies for new worlds to settle. Then enthusiasm waned with the years; the more people strained their eyes at the sky, the less life seemed apparent. Our baseline shifted back. Napier was the exception, not the new rule. It hung there, across the void, A container for all hopes, its atmosphere unsullied with the signature of the civilization that clung heavily and insistently to the Earth.

Trillions of dollars and vast quantities of human capital had gone into the terraforming programme. Plans for Mars, long deemed impractical, were finally retired. The great scientific endeavour of a generation became the settling of human life on a world orbiting a different star. Salzmann's own training in the new interdisciplinary science of terraforming absorbed his entire life. His personality, the thing that had always held him back, finally worked to his advantage.   Then, on Napier, after decades of travel in stasis, they woke up to a toxic rock that alternated between burning and freezing, home to no more life than a thin coating of microbial mats and soupy ponds, respiring limply.

They had been trained to deal with that eventuality; that was what the terraforming programme was for. They were ready to go into stasis again, this time for longer, as the programme executed, seeding Napier's systems with the ingredients of a world fit for large, naked mammals. Salzmann still remembered Nguyen shaking everyone's hand before they went back into their vitrification chambers. He and she had woken up to another nightmare. Everyone else had not.

All along, they could have had this. Underneath their feet, the Earth had been waiting to be reborn. Life – real life, wild and uninhibited – had been hiding in the forgotten places, ready to burst forth and gorge itself on the sun and soil.

So much had been wasted. But now Salzmann was here, and he let the warm wind fill his lungs and the low cries of flying things fill his ears. He felt an energy he had not felt before, his sinews and muscles adapting, reverting to the environment in which his DNA was forged. Everything was gone now, except this. No time, no money, no Assistant Technician Salzmann. He let it all go and let himself be.

The impossibility of it pulled him back. There should have been something – some ruined cities, blasted battlefields, or at least the outlines of roads and fields running across the landscape. Not like this, as if humans had never been here at all. They hadn't been gone that long. He was sure they hadn't.

He shifted on the sand and small stones. It wasn't right that he was here, he knew. It wasn't his place. He should have been glassy and lifeless, entombed with the others. Nothing made him special enough to be here.

Something moved on the other side of the river; something large.

Salzmann stood. He held himself perfectly still, his body tense as taut wire. On the other bank, he saw two shapes emerge from the trees and walk down towards the water. The two creatures were bulky, four-legged, shaggy things. They reached the water and lowered their horned heads to drink; more were joining them now, emerging from the trees. Their soft lowing rode across the river on the wind. He scanned the far treeline, anticipating with a twisted gut the emergence of some cowherd or wrangler.

No-one came. Some of the beasts, their drinking finished, began to wander back towards the forest. They were wild creatures, moving under their own command. Salzmann relaxed for a moment. Then, as the herd hastened back towards the trees, another thought came. Where there were herbivores, there would be carnivores. Instinctively, he threw his head back over his shoulder.

There was nothing there but the gently waving grass and the trees beyond. The sun had gone down, and the humming of insects had quietened. A thrill of fear ran up Salzmann's spine. He gripped his multitool tightly and began to retrace his steps to the lander.

Nguyen was outside, dressed in hazard gear. She held a torch in her right hand, mobbed by a cloud of moths. Something else was in her left hand; Salzmann couldn't make it out in the darkness.

"Where the hell did you go?" she said between her teeth.

"I was surveying."

"You don't just go for a stroll, Salzmann. This is still an Expeditionary Force operation, and I am still in command. Do you understand me?"

She was shaking. He couldn't tell if it was anger, or fear, or something else.

"It's incredible, isn't it?" said Salzmann.

"What did you find?" she asked, suddenly snapping her gaze level.

"Fresh water. And, just...this. So much life."

"Signs of technology?" Her eyebrows arched. He shook his head. He didn't expect her to understand.

"No, nothing. Everything is gone."

She banged a fist against the lander's hull. The noise brought a cloud of small birds fluttering up out of the grass.

"Don't you get it?" Nguyen said. "We could be all that's left."

She looked away from him and leant against the ship, as if she were now making sense of the implications of that fact. The light shifted, and Salzmann realised what she was holding in her other hand. It was her sidearm, a compact titanium pistol. He wondered if he had been in line for a battlefield execution, punishment for the crime of risking his own life.

Nguyen had not left Earth in the same way he had. He had gone to Napier to leave people behind. She had gone there to save them. She had expected to build something new. He decided he should say something.

"Captain," he said, "Just because you were responsible for the deaths of the rest of the crew, I don't think you should worry so much about me. You shouldn't blame yourself that they died, even if you were the responsible person."

Nguyen swivelled around and sunk a heavy blow into his gut with her knee. His breath sucked out and he doubled over into the dewy grass. He reached a hand out to support himself with Nguyen's leg, but she stepped away and let him fall.

"Fuck you, Salzmann," she said. "I didn't fail. You were meant to turn Napier into somewhere we could live. I did my job. I'm still doing it."

Even if Salzmann had wanted to say anything, he had no breath to say it with.

"I'm not giving up," she said. "We're taking this thing back up in the air. We're going to carry on looking. Everything can't just have disappeared."

She stepped back into the lander. The trees and grasses thrummed with the rattling of insect membranes. Above him, the stars wheeled against the blackness.

They had been conducting their aerial survey for forty-eight hours. Nguyen had reverted to her clipped captain's manner, dispensing orders to Salzmann with a studied disinterest as if they were back in the training facility. Salzmann complied in silence. He could still feel her eyes on him, watching as he worked. She seemed to be waiting for him to break the deadlock. Perhaps she wanted an apology. For surviving, for not being someone else. She would be waiting a long time if she did. He was very comfortable keeping his mouth closed.

The survey itself had taught them precisely nothing. Multiple-vector imaging, subsurface scans and all other observations revealed only overgrown wilderness. They gathered resources; organic material to feed into the lander's bioreactor and give the solar cells a rest. The corridors had begun to fill with logs and foliage.

"There is something else we could use as fuel first," he suggested, tilting his head towards the cargo hold.

Nguyen ignored the comment at first, as he expected.

"We're suspending the operation," she said a few minutes later. "The least we can do is give them a final resting place."

The hill she had selected for the crew's barrow was topped with a plateau of copper-tinged soil. As they hacked at it with their entrenching tools, it crumbled into fat, stoneless chunks. Even so, Salzmann felt his body scream at the labour. The stasis-entombment had rendered him brittle, as if the muscles and tendons inside him had fused into a single lump. Nguyen was the same, he could tell, her teeth clenching and the sweat dripping from her back as she worked.

The grass around them writhed with arthropod life, a feast for the chattering squadrons of small birds that danced among the blades. In the distance, herds of herbivores wandered and grazed across the grass. Salzmann felt the red earth cling coldly to his hands, and the heat of the sun on his face. He strained his eyes towards the horizon; at every angle it rolled into mystery, a chaos of growth and twisting earth. Everywhere there was movement in the stillness.

After digging two graves, they took a break. Nguyen went silently back into the lander. Salzmann sat for a few minutes, then began to dig again. He shifted a metre of earth, then stopped. There was something in the soil. It was angular, hard, and inorganic. He stared at it for a moment. His back groaned as he knelt. The object was cold and smooth. Delicately, he shifted more earth away with the tip of his tool. The thing was small; a disc that fit comfortably within the palm of his hand. One surface was irregular with engravings.

The object was undoubtedly metallic. He couldn't be sure of the alloy; some melding of iron, copper, and zinc, he supposed. Around its perimeter ran a string of symbols, in a carefully consistent, blocky lettering. At its centre was a figure, long and bipedal. The broad contours of its face gave it a likeness to a human being.

Nguyen re-emerged from the lander, and he slipped the disc into his pocket. His tongue quivered with intention, but his mouth kept shut. He was sure that Nguyen knew more than she was telling him. Why shouldn't he have a secret of his own?

When Salzmann practised field biology as a student, he had worked with soils that were practically dead, whole clumps falling through his fingers inert and lifeless. Here, the Earth was animated. Every blow into the loamy brown ground brought annelids and isopods to the surface. Their writhing and scuttling delighted him.

The disc sat heavily in his pocket. Like him, it didn't belong here. It was part of an older world that had been swept away. How it had been swept away didn't matter. A new, bountiful era had been born, geological in its ambition. There were no laws and no systems except the swirling gases in the sky and the endless chains of minerals filtering through the Earth.

Soon, within the timescales of this new era, he would rejoin that chain, would become part of that world. Each of the three times Salzmann had gone into stasis, he had been terrified of the process failing, that he would spend eternity as a vitrified husk. Now it felt almost calming when he thought about being down in the Earth, with the worms and ants pulling him apart, along with the rest of the Amritsar's crew.

Nguyen was leaning on her shovel, looking sadly at the bodies in front of her. The ship's pilot, Hernandez, and Chief Technician Gunnersson, Salzmann's old boss. She exhaled deeply.

"I owe you an apology, Salzmann. I haven't reacted well to this. You deserved more of me as your commander. Maybe we can start again?"

He nodded. Even where they were, despite everything, Nguyen was trying to be a leader. It made him feel uncomfortable. She carried on talking.

"You were right, it's incredible. The way life has reasserted itself. Even as a non-specialist I can appreciate that."

"All it needed was for us to get out of the way," he said.

"We'll do better, when we get another chance," she said. He wasn't sure what that meant, but he could tell she wasn't looking for a response. She had something else to say.

"I shouldn't have said what I said. Blamed you for our failure on Napier. That was wrong."

Salzmann shrugged.

"We did fail, though."

"Yes, but not in the way that you think." She looked straight at him. "Our mission to Napier was never about terraforming, not really. Everyone at the strategic level understood that the terraforming technology wasn't advanced enough to succeed, and the chances of finding liveable conditions laughably remote. We were set up to fail."

Salzmann paused to consider this. He had never really believed that the terraforming would be successful, but he had the submissive quality and fatal indifference to trust that his superiors did. It was gratifying to know that he had been right.

"We were always meant to come back here," he said.

Nguyen nodded. "We were an insurance policy for human civilisation on Earth. Napier was a staging post."

It made sense. The Napier system was far enough away. They would lie in stasis for centuries, millennia, as long as it took – letting the terraforming process run in the small chance that it would succeed. Then, when it most probably all went wrong, they would wake up and travel home across the void. They would never know how long they had been asleep.

"You knew this all along?" he asked. He could see irritation work its way back onto Nguyen's face, before she made a conscious effort to wipe it off.

"I knew that things would be different. But I didn't expect everything to be gone so completely. And I thought that there would be more of us." She gestured towards the bodies scattered outside the lander.

Salzmann now understood what she had meant. We'll do better, when we get another chance. Nguyen was a fighter. The mission had faced setbacks, but it was not terminally compromised. She had found the willpower to face up to what must be done. His stomach shifted in unease.

"It's going to get dark again soon," he offered, trying to shift her focus before any more revelations emerged with which he would be required to engage emotionally.

"Should we try to bury a few more of them?"

"I have a better idea." she said.

It took a while to carry each corpse out and pile it at the bottom of the hill. The heap of death was incongruous against the backdrop of the plain; a blot of orderly human destruction soiling the wilderness. Nguyen descended towards it, testing the flame of the plasma torch as she walked.

The funeral pyre lit up quickly and burned with a power that neither of them had expected. They sat and watched the sky grow dark and the flames grow brighter. It was a waste, thought Salzmann, for those bodies to have lasted so long, and now to be disassembled so completely and quickly under the influence of oxygen and heat.

Nguyen and he were both silent. When the pyre had cooled to embers, she rose to go back inside.

He waited for the lander's shutter to close, then carefully pulled the strange metal disc from his pocket. It was dusk and, the light was thin. Hundreds of bats swooped across the sky, their wingbeats a soft pattering. From somewhere – he could not tell if it was near or far – he heard a low feline growl that quivered in his bowels. He moved closer to the lander.

Taking his multitool in an overhand grip, he held the object closer to his face, bringing the text into optimum focus. Salzmann couldn't read it, but he understood something about it. The writing was wrong; not with the neutral meaninglessness of a foreign language, but a quality of deep and burning incomprehensibility. As if he could never understand even the way of understanding it. As if it would not reveal its meaning to him even if he studied it for another hundred thousand years.

A frisson ran over his skin. He held the object at arm's length. From the centre, framed by the impenetrable scrawl, the lanky figure looked up at him. He saw it more clearly now. Its arms were outstretched, its face the three wide circles of two eyes and mouth; somewhere between screaming, questioning, and accusing. It was basic, but not artless or primitive.

Steps rattled on the lander's loading ramp. He slipped the disc back into his pocket. Nguyen was leaning against the entryway. She looked smaller than she had before. She sat down beside him again.

"It's funny," she said, "I knew all along that this was what could happen. I signed up for it, like you said. It wasn't easy, when we woke up on Napier, finding everyone dead except you. I'm a soldier; I dealt with it. But somehow, I thought it wouldn't be just the two of us. That we'd come back, and everything would be like it was before. The future, but the future of a past that I knew."

"It could have been worse," said Salzmann.

"Exactly," she said. She leaned back on the grass, propping herself against a rock. "We could have come back to an asteroid field. Or a radioactive tomb world, or a burning second Venus. But it's not. It's perfect. As if it was waiting for us."

He stayed silent. A stream of decisions and consequences began to suggest itself. The range of possible paths had been broad when they brought the lander down. Now he could hear only one thing in Nguyen's voice. They would start again, like she had said. He saw the lander repurposed into a shelter, solar rigs running at full, rough awnings flying out from hatches propped open. He imagined himself as a hunter, whittling bows and spears and wearing the skins of beasts. The hides of animals splitting under his knife, the blood flowing out and the richest meat torn from the bone.

Nguyen hated him for surviving. She probably always would. Not just because of that, but for who he was, who she was. It wouldn't matter. She had been given a mission and a set of objectives, and she would complete them, even if it meant settling down with Salzmann. His skin prickled at the thought.

The lander had been designed to transport up to twenty individuals; with only two, it was roomy enough for both passengers to have their own quarters and choice of bunks. Compared to the sweeping scale of the world outside, however, it felt to Salzmann like a cell within which he could barely move. He had been worried that Nguyen would try and come in, but she kept her distance, and he lay in silence on the mattress, still in his overalls. As his eyes circled the slats above him, the meaning of things had become clear.

He lowered his hand into his pocket and withdrew the metal disc. He understood what was wrong with it now. He saw the completeness of the cycle. Mankind had already died. Twice, at least, maybe more times than that. The world he had known in the infancy of his now geological lifespan had been wiped from the Earth. From the ashes of that death had risen the unfathomable makers of his disc. Perhaps there had been others in between, coming and going without leaving as much as an artefact. He saw the future. He and Nguyen would be the parents of another epidemic of humanity. Their children and their children's children would multiply; and his descendants would once again strip the world of its life and fatten themselves on its bounty, until the sickness passed, and they too went extinct.

The thought was unbearable, almost bringing tears to his eyes, until his realisation. There was a way he could stop it, if he had the courage. It was in his power.

He left the lander early the next day. Fog was quickly clearing over the plain. It mixed with the charnel ash of the colonists' mass grave to leave a wet smell of death in the air. To the East, in the direction of the rising sun, the plain began to climb into low, forested hills. He headed towards them.

As the sun filled the sky ahead of him, the land began to heat. With it, the chorus of the living planet rose its voice. On top of the constant chatter of birds began to be layered the insistent humming of invertebrate life; and above this the shuffling, grunting mass of the herds that ranged across the plain. He had not appreciated before how far they stretched, only picking out small groups against the waving grasses. He walked for an hour past a single, mixed herd of hoofed beasts. They turned their heads to watch him as he passed.

He thought about the world at it had once been; the lost civilisations that had sprawled vainly across the face of this planet. On the herds of buffalo and antelope he imposed a city, spires and chimney stacks erupting from the plain and stretching towards the clouds, slums and suburbs rolling themselves out across the grasslands like a terrible carpet, flattening all life before them. Over the din of the wilderness he recalled his faint memory of the city's sounds; the voices of humans and machines raised against each other in permanent anger. He imagined the air thick with particulate matter and the water slick with oils, a cocktail of nitrates pumped clean of life. It could happen again, he thought. Because of him, it could happen again.

He looked back across the plain. The lander, perched on its mound, was just a point through the haze of the shimmering heat. He wondered if Nguyen was still asleep.

"I'm sorry" he said aloud, into the savannah.

He began to walk again. The forest began to close around him, stifling the sun and softening sound. At a narrow stream, he stopped. He tossed his multitool into the water and watched it sink and roll along with the current, knocking against rocks and branches. Then he carried on. The ground rose. He scrambled upwards over rocks, scrabbled up banks.

He had known what he had to do since last night. Now it began to seem real; or at least as real as it ever could. If it had all been down to him to do it, he would not have been able to. But there was something easy about this way. He just needed to keep walking, and nature would follow its timeless pattern.

He wasn't sure that he understood what he was doing any better than Nguyen would. But every breath he took of the life-drenched atmosphere, every footstep that sent small things scurrying into the shadows; they were all the argument he needed. This was how the world was meant to be. There was only one thing that was wrong. He was in it. They were in it.

The moment came quicker than he expected. In a clearing, the shape was hunched and mottled against the trees; by the time he was close enough to see it, it was too late to do anything, even if he had wanted to. It had probably been following him for hours. The feline shape, coiled and muscular, brought a clanging peal of fear from his genetic memory. It was aggressively real, the vegetation parting around it.

The leopard's low growl echoed through his organs. For a minute it stood still, watching him and waiting, ears twitching. It took one pace forward, then another. Then it began to move; accelerating in seconds from statue-still to death dash. It hit Salzmann like an asteroid colliding with a young moon. Instinct took control, writhing and screaming, sending the forest around him into panicked flight. As everything around him ended, he saw and smelt the earth, rich and red with his blood. He would be a part of it again.

See Matt Hornsby's story "A Final Resting Place" online at Metaphorosis.
If you liked it, leave a comment. Authors love that!
Remember to subscribe to our e-mail updates so you'll know when new stories are posted.

About the story

This story came together from a couple of different ideas I had. I remember reading 'The World Without Us' by Alan Weisman around the time of a train journey I took across Hungary and Romania, and looking out the window at the landscape — already much wilder than anything in the UK — and imagining it returned to nature completely in the absence of humans, a kind of European Serengeti. Would we recognise such a place, or would it be completely alien? At the same time I was thinking a lot about a central question in environmental ethics, about the value of the living world in the absence of intelligent beings like us to perceive it. That was a couple of years ago, and with the growing volume of concern about environmental breakdown, it feels more relevant. Which is lucky for me, if not for anyone else!

I also wanted to create a distinctive voice for the main character — Salzmann — that was almost uncomfortably analytical, to the extent that mundane observations of the natural world can feel eerie and disturbing. I think some of Jeff Vandermeer's protagonists were a strong model for this, in the

Southern Reach trilogy and 'Borne'. I'm not sure I pulled it off, but that's what I was going for.

Everything else just sort of filtered in from other influences as I was writing it. In any case, I hope it's a good read!

A question for the author

Q: Aliens. Are they out there?

A: I've never been able to decide on this, but at the moment I am leaning towards yes, although quite possibly in some format that we would find quite disappointing or incomprehensible. Certainly no Klingons or beautiful green women. Arthur C. Clarke said, either we are alone in the universe or we are not, and either way the answer is terrifying - but it's also quite amazing.

About the author

Matt Hornsby is based between London, United Kingdom, and Dublin, Ireland. When not writing, he works on environmental and economic policy, after previous lives as a scrap metal dealer and English teacher. Follow him on twitter at @MatthOrnsby.

The Guardian of Werifest Park

Carly Racklin

The train car reeked of cigarettes and rumbled like a storm. Loud enough to drown out the voice of every passenger crammed inside it, but still Inez's heartbeat rattled between her ears. It had started when she stuffed her backpack with clothes in the dark, and only boomed louder as she'd slipped out past her mother's wheezy, sleeping form on the couch, thirty-six or so hours earlier.

It had followed her through the cracked streets, then onto the bus, and all five trains after that. Or was it six, now? She hadn't slept a wink since the drumming started. She'd begun to think nothing would ever be quiet again.

The bruise on her cheek had faded enough now to be mistaken for a shadow on dusky skin, though it throbbed faintly in time with her pulse. No one had even spared her a passing glance when she boarded the train.

Inez had wedged herself into a far, windowless crevice of a seat, clutched her backpack hard against her chest, and waited for the dread to loosen its grip.

No luck yet. So onward it was.

Once her current train clanked into the station, she shuffled onto the platform and took a deep breath, only to taste even more bitterness in it. She reached into her pocket and drew out less than a dollar in change.

"Shit."

Strangers shoved past her and onto their trains. The longer she stood staring at those coins, the louder the dread rumbled in her skull. She needed to keep moving.

She drifted across the sprawl of washed-out tile, out of the paths of others who searched the flickering TV screens beseechingly. Everyone she passed was going in the opposite direction from her.

Inez stepped out into the stale summer air and walked. She walked until the afternoon bled into dusk and the day wasted away under the heels of her second-hand sneakers. She wove through gray streets flanked by gray buildings wearing more gray smoke like scarves. The hollow chill thickened in her gut with each step against the hard sidewalk, but she slogged on.

There had to be *something*. Something, not anything. No shelters—she wasn't a stray. A church could work. Hell, she'd take a bench at this point. Anything would do, so long as it wasn't that house.

Unlike her mother, Inez knew when to quit. When to give a place over to the vermin wasting it. The situation turned out to be comically simple, really. In the end, it all boiled down to a choice. Get out, or get wiped out.

Inez kept walking. Her stomach kept roaring, and her heart drummed on and on and on.

Then, the trees.

So many trees, all soft edges and swaying and green. An ocean of trees stretched to the sky and down the block and farther, farther than bleary eyes could measure. The first real trees she'd seen in days, wearing a collar of what was probably the sorriest excuse for a fence in the entire world. Inez jogged across the street and approached a large, slightly crooked sign.

TRESPASSERS WILL BE PROSECUTED.

The words were printed in bold black type and hung against a background that at some point must have been white.

PARK HOURS: 7AM-7PM.

The last dregs of sunset fell yellow and molten over the skin of her neck and the heavy padlock on the gate. Inez glanced over her shoulder to the city. Just looking at it made her itch to take a puff of her inhaler she knew she couldn't spare. No telling when she'd be able to refill her prescription again.

Despite the heat, Inez shivered, and a whisper from somewhere deep and dark in her chest asked, *What were you thinking?*

Behind her, the street was miraculously clear of cars. For one floating, dream-still moment, the only things breathing were her and those trees. Rustling, watching. Waiting to see what she would do.

She ignored the voice and climbed the fence.

Her feet hit the earth with a soft thud. She tore off her shoes and stuffed them into her backpack, sighing as grass eased the concrete's ache from her soles. Another sign accosted her a few strides in, this one so eroded it seemed ancient, hanging around the trunk of a tree like an amulet: a thirty-one point list of the park's prohibited activities. Vines and moss skirted its edges, entwined in the gaps of the chain that held it aloft.

No smoking, no hunting, no trapping, no littering, no fishing in the pond, no carving the trees, no, no, no. They would have saved a lot of paint if they'd just written KEEP YOUR DAMN HANDS TO YOURSELF. Inez wondered if there were security cameras in the park, but that would involve breaking about four of their own rules.

She ambled on until the fence disappeared from view. There weren't even any real footpaths, just vague stretches of faded grass, mostly concealed by the shells of parched leaves. *No digging. No vehicles.* Sounds of the city beyond waned with every step until they were barely memories. The dulcet crooning of unseen birds replaced the din of construction, of razing machinery. No sign of the skyscrapers, no sign of a single gray thing.

Huckleberries dotted the dark brush. Inez plucked them up in clusters as she walked, barely chewing, her relief turning even the most unripe clumps nectarous and intoxicating.

The path curved, and around the bend stood an enormous weeping willow. Under it: a bench. For the first time in weeks, maybe months, Inez laughed.

She sat down, shucked off her backpack, and took deep, even breaths. The air tasted sweeter than the berries.

But her clothes still smelled of her mother's cigarettes. So did the backpack, and the short dark coils of her hair. Now, though, in this park, the bitter smell seemed to have dissipated a little. Like the fresh air was washing her clean from the inside out.

Dusk elapsed in minutes; night draped the trees in obsidian. With the dark and stillness and her newly full stomach came syrupy fatigue. It colored everything—even the dingy bench was transformed into the softest and warmest bed she had known in years. For a long time, the only thing she did was breathe, letting herself sink further into the summer air, and it into her.

With every inhale, she imagined it purifying the black secondhand-smoke stains in her lungs, then sneaking into her veins and her brain, erasing every ugly thing that lived there, every memory molding in every dark corner and inside every wall.

Yes, she was alone in a city she didn't know the name of, broke and bedding down on a park bench. And there was a stubborn weight in her chest that she couldn't ignore, and bruises still clinging to her skin. But there were wild berries too, and trees tall enough to blot out the sky, and she didn't have to think of her mother ever again. For now, that would have to be enough.

The willow leaves rustled loudly above her, though the air was still. Inez couldn't bring herself to open her eyes again once they fell closed. So she just listened, and after a while, the rustling ceased.

She couldn't remember the last time she'd slept in air this clean, or the last time she'd lain in the night without listening to her mother slinking in the door with her latest fix. It was a different world entirely, a world made only of crisp, bright things. Balmy green things her mother's smoke could never spoil.

Inez slept like the dead, and dreamt of nothing at all. Until a sharp rattling cut through the gloom and jolted her awake into a dry early dawn.

For a moment the world reeled and her head spun, full of dizzy white flickers. She was stuck between spinning and floating, half numb still from the previous day's exhaustion. The rattling continued, and Inez jerked up from the bench when she recognized it as the sound of the metal fence.

The sun had just barely begun to light the park, like the first translucent strokes of an underpainting. What could it be, six in the morning? No way anyone was opening that gate right now.

But she hadn't needed to open the gate to get in.

The heavy crunch of footsteps sounded from nearby.

"Shit!" Inez hissed, and in a frantic blur, snatched up her backpack and dove for cover behind the thick trunk of the willow tree.

The footsteps lurched slowly nearer, down the same path she'd taken to the bench, and on. When they passed the tree, Inez held her breath, and leaned just slightly out into the open to regard her fellow trespasser.

Square shoulders, baggy jeans, dusty combat boots. The man plodding past couldn't have been much older than her, judging by his height and clothes. He stomped listlessly through the grass, clutching an aluminum can. Drunk.

He stopped walking a few feet past the bench. A lit cigarette teetered between the fingers of his free hand. He took a swig from the can, then a puff from the cigarette. The cloud of gray smoke he breathed into the air caused a queasy flutter in Inez's chest. Moments later, the scent hit her, and despite how hard she tried to fight it off, she couldn't breathe.

She hadn't smelled such strong cigarettes since her mother last lit one. That night could have been a lifetime ago, for how far away it felt. Ever since she was a little girl, any fresh whiff of that bitter smoke, and she was gasping, looking for fire, looking for ruin. She'd woken from nightmares of her mother turned to nothing but a heap of char on that ratty couch too many times to count.

When she was fourteen, the doctor had diagnosed her with asthma and recommended nicotine gum to her mother. And every night since for three whole years, Inez had slept with her window open and door shut.

Just when she thought she'd found the one place on earth where that smell couldn't follow her.

The man took another drag, his head lolling back with the inhale. Then he flicked the cigarette away, and it fell to the earth. The ashy end of it sputtered against the brittle foliage. Inez knew what came next, but when the orange flickers caught and burst outwards, she gasped as if she were the one burned.

The stranger whirled about. His glazed-over eyes met hers. Inez trembled and flinched, dropping back from her haunches into the dirt. Smoke drifted up from the ground in a thin curl.

A splitting thrum cut through the air. It sent a stabbing pain through the base of her skull, so loud it could have been coming from inside the bone. Like the whole forest had just trembled with her.

The willow tree above her shook violently again, without even a whisper of a breeze. The drunk man was not looking at her anymore, but up at the tree.

She followed his gaze to the branches. They weren't where she remembered them being.

The boughs bent to the ground, splayed apart wide like fingers. Inez took a breath that froze in her throat. Then the trunk of the willow tree uprooted from the earth.

It was much quieter than she would have ever guessed—to hear a tree tear itself out of the ground. For a moment, there was only a hum. Then a sharp crackle rippled through the stillness, and the trunk split in two. The halves met the ground, looking like the lean brown legs of a Titan. On either side of the tree, the remaining branches twisted into coils. Green vines dangled in a tight, roundish cluster at the willow's crest: a faceless head glistening with dew.

Inez had barely heaved in a new breath when the tree-thing angled its colossal semblance of a body toward the drunk man. At his feet, the cigarette still sputtered, glowing like a shrunken sun but giving no life. It would drain the green from anything it touched.

A yowl, like the groaning of a twig right before it snaps, sounded from the bundle of leaves atop the tree. It stuck in Inez's ears, in her teeth, in her ribs. It clashed with the piercing blare that the lit cigarette had conjured and for all she knew they were the same thing. Maybe that was what everything sounded like when you were going to die.

Inez's body moved separate from her mind. She crawled toward the cigarette on her hands and knees, and the willow moved too, overtaking her in one heaving stride. The drunk man had already started to run.

The whole world was rattling and that cigarette was still burning in the grass, like her mother, poisoning everything, and she couldn't breathe. She had to make it stop. In her peripheral vision the tree creature continued to move, its gnarled limbs cleaving through the air.

Inez mirrored it, throwing out her arm and smothering the cigarette against her hand. Ahead of her the creature halted, one of its branches seizing up mid-swing. The man disappeared into the brush and out of sight. When the metal fence jangled sharply in the distance not long after, the creature lowered its arm.

Inez's vision blurred. Panic pounded in her skull, almost loud enough to drown out the giant's gait as it turned back and thumped toward her.

Her chest burned with emptiness. She fumbled in her pocket for her inhaler. Blackness choked every thought in her head except the ones steering her hands.

Nothing left to exhale. *Click. Hiss.* Breathe in—hold—breathe out.

It took three puffs for the vise around her lungs to loosen. The world came slowly back into focus with every heave, centering on an ugly red burn glaring up from the center of her palm.

A tall shadow crashed over her. Inez looked up, breath thin again.

The creature had no eyes to meet but its stare still pierced. It stood rigid, a monument of bristled greenery. Tears welled up in Inez's eyes. Either from fear or pain, she wasn't sure. It didn't really matter, because she was going to die any second now. The creature craned its verdant body downward as if in confirmation.

Inez snapped her head down, closed her eyes, and waited to be crushed. Waited like she had those nights ago, back pressed to her bedroom door as it rattled with the force of her mother's fists, the air bloated with cigarette smoke and a voice screaming out for her blood.

She'd thought her mother was still sleeping off her latest bender when she flushed the pills. But her hands just wouldn't stop shaking, and everything had clattered to the floor, and she'd only gotten a few handfuls down the pipes when fingers had twisted into her hair and wrenched her back. A hand had crashed against her cheekbone, knocking her into the wall. Her ears rang and her mother had slipped on the tile, so Inez ran. She'd locked herself in her room and wept until long after her mother had given up on threatening to strangle her.

She'd made her decision before the latch even clicked. The next time she ran would be the last.

Curled in on herself in the dirt, Inez let the tears fall. Choked whimpers leaked through her teeth, clenched tight against the smoke. It could have been her mother there, all smoldering ash. Geared to snuff her out like an ember into a cracked tray.

Inez waited to die.

And waited. And waited.

Something soft brushed down her cheek. She gasped and the aroma of damp foliage flooded her mouth.

Rustling surrounded her. A faint creaking joined it, lurking just beneath the steady hum of leaves. Alike in timbre to what had sounded in the chaos, but with none of the venom—the same voice, a different tone. She blinked the tears out of her eyes. The green mop of vines hung just a few inches from her face, the rest of the creature bent in an awkward, jointless attempt at kneeling.

It didn't crush her. Instead, it raised one of the branches from its side and took her gingerly by the wrist of her burned hand. The long sprigs of leaves drew open her fist. This time, the noise that rose from the creature's unseen mouth was nearly a chirp, the pitch of it leaping, like a question. Shrill with curiosity, maybe even concern.

Before she could dwell on how pathetic that thought was, the giant punctuated its remark with a tilt of its massive leafy head, and sparks stirred in Inez's skull.

It was *talking* to her.

She searched for any hint of eyes behind those vines. "I . . . um, I don't understand," she muttered, unsteady with the new weight of this wonder. But it was true: she was still alive, and a beast dressed in forestry had really just materialized because someone burned the grass.

She looked to the gray smudge between the two of them, where the extinguished cigarette lay, then at her palm, cradled by the willow's wispy fingers. "It burned you too."

The vines around her hand drew upwards a fraction, and a thin stream of clear water trickled out from a fissure in the branch and washed over her ash-dotted palm. She flinched and hissed at the sting.

The willow made a cooing noise that sounded an awful lot like the calming hums other people's mothers made to their fussy children. Had it learned that from observation? Or did nature have its own language of tenderness?

"Thank you," Inez said, brushing her fingers over the bark.

Again that rustling echoed around them, and the giant let her go. It rose with a chorus of creaks and trod heavily back toward the patch of ragged earth behind the bench.

Sunlight broke through the canopy and gilded the grass so fiercely Inez had to squint. Soundlessly, the earth began to knit itself back together once the rooted feet of the willow settled into the hollow they'd created. Time seemed to move in reverse as its limbs unwound and stretched to their original shape. By the time she blinked the brightness away, the bench and willow tree stood perfectly undisturbed, the burn in her palm the only indicator that any of it had ever happened.

Inez pushed herself up on two wobbly legs and teetered over to the tree, a small grin fighting its way across her face. She hitched her toppled backpack onto her shoulder; it weighed practically nothing now. One errant breeze and she might just float away like a petal, sheer and light enough to never touch the ground again.

That didn't sound so bad.

When she was just a little girl, 'never' had been the scariest word in the world. A cage that would suffocate her if she got too close. But now, 'never' was more secure than anywhere. Not a cage, but armor. She could lie down inside it and it would keep her safe.

Never was a survivor's word.

She'd whispered it in the din of every train, to the dread each time it returned and choked the breath from her chest— *never, never, never.* She was never going back.

And the dread was quieter now, like she'd finally gone far enough.

Inez rubbed her fingertips gratefully over the knobs and valleys in the willow's bark.

Someone would be opening that gate soon. If she were careful, she could get out before anyone knew she'd entered at all. She would be anonymous again.

Anonymous, but not free. Not free of the dread, or the smoke, or the exhaustion of searching for hope in a colorless city.

At least this place had rules. Rules meant care, and she'd seen precious little of that for a long, long time.

Inez pressed her ear to the willow. She didn't know what she expected to hear, but when it was silent, she couldn't stop her heart from sinking.

"Hello?" she mumbled, and rapped against the wood lightly with her knuckles. "Are you still there? I, um, didn't realize this park was already occupied." Her chuckle came out crumpled like the leaves dappling the undergrowth. No reaction. Maybe it was sleeping. Maybe it just wanted her to shut up and leave it alone. Or maybe it didn't care about her at all, so long as she didn't break any of the rules.

Leaving it be seemed like the safest bet. She didn't want to test the limits of its hospitality, not after what she'd just witnessed.

Feeling childish and yet vaguely like she was being watched, Inez started off in a new direction, away from the pseudo-footpath she'd first followed and into the brush. The noisy layers of expired leaves crackled like tinder with each stride.

By late morning, the air swelled with heat. She downed one of the water bottles she'd had the good sense to buy during her train-hopping, and had half-stuffed the empty plastic shell into her backpack when the sound of real running water hit her, muffled a little by distance. She followed it until her bare feet pushed through a hedge and slipped into blessedly cool mud.

A thin stream wound through the clearing. On its bank, hundreds of yellow flowers gleamed from spray cast off the rocks. Inez propped her backpack up against a tree, sat down on the edge of the brook and dipped her legs into the cool, glossy water. She splashed a handful over her face and scrubbed the scum of the last few days away.

Sighing, she shut her eyes and lay back against the bed of flowers. Her fingers carded through their velvety leaves, tight and tangled like her own curls. Her head went woozy with the blossoms' sweet scent.

She listened for any sounds of the city, knowing it lurked on all sides of the park. Still nothing. If the skyscrapers were teeth, then this forest sat in the middle of a wide-open jaw, surrounded on all sides but never devoured.

Something was different here—she'd noticed it before, but not realized how deep the sensation ran. It wasn't just the air, or the trees, or the ground. It was everything.

Her thoughts drifted again to that list of rules. It hung in her mind in the same looming way it hung on its tree, fixed in place even by the foliage. Different from everything else, but not unwelcome.

Inez opened her eyes, and swallowed a yelp. A figure hovered over her, though that was all she could really call it. Its vaguely human-shaped body was comprised entirely of clustered leaves and budded flowers. It seemed to watch her, though the closest thing to eyes it possessed were two blossoms just slightly larger than the rest, fixed at the middle of its lumpy crown.

She sat up and turned around to face the thing. Its maybe-head followed her. It looked like some kind of artsy hedge trimming from a magazine. Like someone had tried to haphazardly sculpt a person out of foliage, someone who didn't know for sure, or didn't care to know, exactly what people looked like.

"Oh, there are more of you," Inez blurted, heart still racing. Rustling filled her head. She held up her burnt hand and gave a short wave.

The leaves on the creature shook slightly, back and forth.

Inez worked her bottom lip between her teeth. "No? You're . . . just one?" She gestured over her shoulder back toward the general direction of the willow.

Another hum, then all the flower buds on the creature's body bloomed into striking tiny suns. The blossoms skirting the stream repeated the display, petals flaring out in a long wave. Warmth so far from the summer's unflinching aridity saturated the air; she breathed in and felt it in her chest, searching for soil to take root in.

Inez smiled, and caressed the leaves below her again. The little red dot glared up from her palm beneath the vegetation, a reminder of the damage already done, how they'd both been burned. A handful of soft gestures wouldn't erase that.

But it was better than nothing. Or so she hoped.

Inez watched the creature watching her, and wondered if it felt her touch like it had felt the cigarette. Maybe it felt everything the forest did, every inch of every acre. Like veins, connecting each life to the next, tying blade of grass to sprawling tree to sunning flower, each to each to each. A system, and its heart. What a thing to share a wound with.

"Those rules back there are yours, aren't they? They were written for you," she said.

Thirty-one rules was nothing compared to all the ways a thing could be hurt. All the ways a life could be snuffed out. No death too small to grieve. Like it ignored no offense, no wrong. Carrying a memory as old as earth.

Inez saw it all again: the cigarette, and the man, and the creature's arm raised knifelike in the air. A threat, and a response. She'd only seen it respond like that once, but judging by that sign, she guessed it had happened before, and often, who knew how long ago. How many small wars had the creature waged before someone had taken pity on it and written the restrictions that hung over the place?

Too many, of course. It was always too many.

The sun retreated and plunged the bank into shadow. She looked up, but found her vision swimming. The creature was closer now, an unreadable blur of gold and green. Inez shuddered under its unyielding stare. Her smile grew heavy on her face, and fell away without a sound.

She peeled her limbs away from the flowerbed and stood. Papery yellow petals came away with her, stuck with sweat to her skin. The moments of her life from before then unspooled behind her eyes, faded by time but still clinging like old stains to the fabric of her memory. She didn't want them.

Her heart pounded. "Do you want me to leave?" Inez asked in a small voice.

The creature gave no response. The warmth in her chest turned sour.

"Do you?" she said, louder now, though a shameful crack in her voice split the word. Dread wormed a cold trail through her. She didn't need an answer to know it was true, but the miserable reality of it hollowed out her chest. She swallowed down a sob.

The creature's form shrank back at the accusation, all of its flowers returned to buds.

It wouldn't have been the first thing to want her gone. Wouldn't have been the first place better off without her.

Inez knew pity when she saw it. It looked just like disdain, but with a prettier face.

She stumbled back a step, then another, until the hedge she'd first emerged from brushed her ankles.

She really hadn't learned anything, had she?

"I'm sorry," she mumbled. Her feet scrabbled for purchase on uneven ground. "I just wanted—I just—"

Inez turned and ran. The tears finally fell as she lurched through the bushes, over brittle grass and twigs that jabbed like needles. Each one another twist of the knife, a reminder of what she had known before ever climbing that fence but had refused to admit.

She didn't belong here.

But it was worse than that, and she knew it. She didn't belong anywhere.

A root smacked her ankle, and Inez tumbled into the dirt with a weak yelp of pain. Every heaving of her breath scorched like swallowing a red-hot sword. She pushed herself up on limp arms. Stinging outside and in, she clambered backwards until she hit a tree's gnarled trunk, decked in winding dark leaves. Then she hugged her knees to her chest and wept into her hands.

She wished the earth would just swallow her up. If she could just bury all her deluded fantasies and dissolve into the soil, maybe something good and useful would finally grow out of her, something that deserved to be there in that fence, a part of that system.

Loved. Or worth loving, anyway.

And that was just it.

The nameless weight beneath Inez's ribs swelled and flooded her chest with a gloom blacker than her mother's lungs.

She couldn't breathe, again. She fished out her inhaler from her pocket and took a puff, barely able hold it steady. The last time she'd triggered an attack from crying had been the night she flushed the drugs. She could almost smell the smoke again. Could still feel the grain of her bedroom door grate against her shuddering back.

Her breath returned in gasps, a thousand aches with it.

Just barely, on the edge of the forest's din, Inez heard rustling. The foliage beneath her shook.

A whorl of vines crept away from trunk and curled around her, covered in enormous scarlet roses. The mass encircled her in moments, overflowing with the balmy scent of petals. She gasped, and a rose-dappled vine reached out and swept over her bruised cheek, wiping away the last tear still inching down through the grime.

Something had grabbed hold of her lungs again, and her heart too, and held them with such puzzling fortitude and tenderness that Inez thought she would weep again.

The mass of vines and roses embraced her. Softly and resolutely. Tenderly and fiercely. The way her mother used to, before everything went wrong. She'd forgotten what it felt like.

She exhaled and sank into the creature's arms. Links of thornless blooming vine cradled her, stroking her hair in the same smooth motions her hands had used in the patch of flowers back by the stream.

"Why are you doing this?" she whispered. "I'm just the same as them."

A low hum reverberated from deep in the petals, but Inez couldn't decipher its meaning. The creature only held her tighter when she made no reply.

Inez breathed until the pain in her throat subsided to a faint prickling numbness. She wanted to lie down until she remembered nothing of her mother or the gray-stained house she'd run from. But the memories clung to her bones like weeds. She wondered if she would ever be able to uproot them without also uprooting herself. If she would ever be as green and blooming and free as the things that held her inside the fence.

Hesitantly, Inez reached into the leaves and returned the embrace.

The creature's silken-edged form stiffened, then recoiled. The climbing roses and vines receded, slumping limp against the trunk.

By the time she'd gasped and called out brokenly after it, the creature was already gone. Inez stood. Confusion struck her first, then cold terror. Something was wrong. Goosebumps mottled her bare arms and legs. She stared hollowly into the horizon for a long time.

When a breeze blew, she tasted smoke on it.

Not the bitter tobacco, lung-rotting stuff. Worse. The kind that swallowed houses and skin. The kind that cooked.

Inez went rigid. All the green around her swayed as one vast wall, revealing almost nothing. No more than a few slivers of sky to search, and no sign of the stench's source.

"Move, just *move*," she spat at her quaking knees. "Where are you?" she cried up at the trees.

No answer.

Then, voices. Men's voices, the words turned garbled and staticky by distance. The murmurs became yelling, and by the time Inez had turned in their direction, three men careened out of the trunks' thick barricade.

They nearly barreled into her, but the one leading the charge skidded to a stop

just inches in front of Inez. His scuffed combat boots kicked up a small cloud of dirt.

A flock of birds scattered noisily from the treetops.

"Holy shit," he whispered. Inez flinched at the rancid booze on his breath. "It's you."

Two others crowded at his back. They could have been triplets, for their shared tawny hair and pasty white faces. A lopsided tattoo of a tiger stared directly at her from one's bare shoulder.

Inez blinked, unable to call any words to her tongue.

"I told you someone else was there," Combat Boots said over his shoulder with a laugh. He stepped toward her, and she stumbled back in turn. Her pulse boomed in her ears.

"Who cares, dude? Let's get the hell out of here," interjected one of the others, grasping his friend by the shoulder and giving it a good shake. Shaggy hair obscured most of his face, except for a lip ring that glinted in the sun.

Combat Boots laughed louder. His right hand clutched an open lighter, the flame thrashing.

All the warmth drained out of Inez.

"I was right. All along—about everything, I was right. What do you think of that, assholes?" he howled, turning on his heels. Inez barely ducked out of the lighter's arc.

Tiger Tattoo stepped aside. "You're out of your damn mind!" he scoffed. "I'm not about to die here."

The smell of the smoke was stronger now. Past the undulating trees, Inez thought she glimpsed a smudge of gray. "What did you do?" she muttered, slack-jawed.

She took another step back, but Combat Boots swung around and seized her wrist. She yelped; his bony fingers held deceptively strong.

"Let go of me." She tugged hard, but he clamped down harder. "*Ow*—stop! Let *go!*"

A tremor traveled up her legs from the ground.

Lip Ring and Tiger Tattoo glanced at each other, then broke out running, following their original course into the treeline.

Another tremor, then another. Softly, in the back of her skull, a familiar hum sounded.

"You know I'm right. You were right there with me," Combat Boots ranted, pressing his pale, pocked face in close.

Inez had readied a leg to kick him where it would hurt, when thundering footsteps broke in. The air smelled like death.

The treeline shattered open.

Inez barely recognized the willow. Swirling fire engulfed its extremities, each wispy vine a wick. Dark billows rose thickly from its upper half. It looked hasty, incomplete, the trunk barely divided enough for movement. It limped forward, and each ungainly step filled the air with a cacophony of dreadful cracks. Behind it, a trail of red and black cut into the park as far as Inez could see.

The air was kindling.

She wanted to scream, but her lips formed useless shapes around nothing and made no sound. Combat Boots' grin melted away. He released her arm and ran.

The willow screeched, heaving after him. One leg splintered apart as soon as it met earth, and the whole creature teetered, then came crumpling thunderously down. Breathless, she couldn't call out for it.

Embers flew, swallowing the brittle foliage in a flood of char. The willow craned the blackened remains of its head down and made a high, broken sound, then collapsed in a tide of cinders.

Tears and smoke burned Inez's eyes. She whipped around and around, but couldn't find the trees, or the sky, or the creature. Ash coated her tongue and crept down her throat no matter how she coughed. She fell to her knees and wheezed helplessly.

Everything was falling apart again.

Nowhere to run. The air was red, her sweat was red, her thoughts were red.

There was a choice, a choice. What was it?

Inez reached for her inhaler.

Get out—

But it was gone.

—or get wiped out.

Darkness descended. It swallowed her whole and washed away the scorched clearing. A rough and solid slab slipped under her legs and hoisted her up, and up, and up from the ground. She scrabbled for balance, gasping weakly. Her fingertips scraped bark.

Cracks of light revealed the mass shielding her: a thick canopy of leaves.

Inez reached out to touch them, and her inhaler fell into her palm with a muted thump. She took two doses. On her first good breath she tasted foliage, then hacked out black dust.

The tree lurched into motion. The branch beneath her shifted and nestled her against the upper part of the trunk. She heard the distant crackle of fire, and vaguely smelled the smoke. More than anything she felt the rocking of the tree, of the giant as it walked, cradling her against its bulk.

Lost for words, she took deep, grateful breaths of the mossy bark. Tears streamed through the dust on her face, over her cracked lips, and onto the tree.

She was alive.

Seconds or minutes or hours passed before the creature creaked to a halt, and Inez's forehead lightly smacked its rough flesh. The limb that held her curled up and drew her away from the trunk.

Air crashed over her. The shield of leaves unraveled and bared her to the sunlight. She blinked, and saw the chugging smoke leaking from the center of the park, how glowing fire split the trees with crimson light. For a moment she soared, weightless, against the bleeding sky. Then the branch that bore her stretched and tilted. She slipped from bark to concrete.

Sidewalk chilled her feet. A shape heaved through the air and smacked the pavement: her backpack.

The creature pulled away, back toward the burning forest.

Inez howled with every last shard of herself, "*No!*" She shot forward, fingers grasping the rusted fence.

The creature's limbs groaned as it withdrew, unheeding. Fear thundered in her skull. She hauled herself halfway up the fence in an instant, until the tree turned back to her in a creaking blur. Bark met her shoulders, leaves pried her fingers open. Together they pushed her, struggling, back down to the pavement.

Sirens resounded from the verging streets.

"Don't go back in there." she rasped, fresh tears stinging in her eyes.

This couldn't be happening. It couldn't save her just to disappear again. She was so tired of being left, of being alone.

"It's too late. You'll burn."

The creature replied something just as broken. Still, it pushed her to the sidewalk.

"Don't, please. Stay with me," she cried, clutching the branch and tugging it closer. Leaves caressed her face.

The giant murmured quietly and pressed itself into her hands for just a moment, then pulled away. Behind the fence, the creature turned and stomped back into the forest as fire engines pulled up on the street, and Inez wept, drowned out by the sirens.

When figures began to pour from the trucks, she scrambled across the street and deposited herself on a bench beside a dried-up fountain. Flocks of chattering onlookers crowded at the fence as the minutes drew on and smoke stole the color from the sky. None spoke to her, and she didn't speak to them.

Once she turned her back to the park, and the fire, and all the clamor of the scene, she didn't look back. She wouldn't.

It was what she'd done when she left her mother. She made her choice and knew not to turn around, but not because she'd go back if she did. She couldn't look back and move forward at the same time. She had to choose. So she chose running. She chose a future, just like she'd done before.

Dread and shame roiled together in her chest. She'd had no right to beg a guardian to abandon its duty, its home, for her. She was nobody.

She'd been so naïve, thinking that running away was the same as escaping. The same as healing. But distance had nothing to do with it. There was no escaping the past, just learning to carry it.

Her mother, that house, they were just memories. Soon the park would be too. There were so many hollow places in her now; she had more than enough room to keep them safe. She could carry them forever.

Inez sat quietly for a long time. Then she put on her shoes and walked to the train station.

Inside, the building was even colder than before, with polished floors that squeaked with every footfall. She passed at least ten TVs, their screens all flashing red, alternating headlines reading, FIRE IN OLD LANDMARK WERIFEST PARK. AUTHORITIES RESPONDING TO REPORTS OF UNIDENTIFIED FIGURE SEEN WITHIN.

Groups huddled beneath the television sets, their eyes squinted, gesturing emphatically at the footage of the fire, but

Inez was too far away to see what captivated them. They paid no mind to her or her ash-caked clothes.

She washed herself clean in a bleached white bathroom. The soap smelled harsh and fruity, and it erased the must of scorched earth from her skin. When at last she scrubbed at the tracks her tears had left in the dirt on her face, the door squealed across the tile, and a woman walked in.

Contorted over the sink, Inez froze, and the stranger did too. She was blonde, with ivory skin, and wore a red pantsuit. Her eyes examined Inez with scalpel sharpness for only a second, then softened to glimmering amber.

Droplets of lukewarm water ran down Inez's chin and puddled on the floor. The woman's hands flexed around the handle of her purse. In a saccharine voice that could only belong to a teacher of small children, she asked, "Are you all right, dear?"

"Yeah," Inez said.

"Are you sure?"

She wiped her chin. "Yeah."

The woman's lipstick was the color of freshly bloomed roses. "Do you . . . need anything? Is there anything I can do for you?"

"Yeah."

The woman bought her a ticket for the train. When asked where she wanted to go, all Inez could think to say was, "Somewhere green, with no fences." No more skyscrapers, no more smoke, and no more living things in cages. She was sick of suffocating.

They stood together on the platform afterward, and Inez thanked her, clutching her ticket. The woman just smiled, nodded, and pressed her hand on Inez's shoulder briefly. She watched the slight jerk of the woman's eyes as they flickered between her face and the news still playing on the TV behind her.

She expected some kind of warning. A *"be careful out there"* or, *"take care of yourself."* But all she said was, "The world is a very big place, you know. It's easy to get lost in."

But it's not, Inez wanted to say. *It's not. It's very small. And everything burns just the same everywhere. Burns again, and again, and again. The only thing that changes is who gets blamed.*

No words came. The woman smiled blankly, then turned and left, and so did Inez.

Practically deserted, the train started off with a metallic screech the moment Inez sat down. She let her backpack slide off her shoulders. A tunnel swallowed the car in darkness, and sleep stole her away before the light returned.

When she woke, the train was still moving, but the city was long gone. The woman had slipped her some extra cash before leaving, which she'd spent on a ridiculously expensive sandwich at the nearest food cart to her track. She scarfed the whole thing down in huge, graceless bites. Her stomach soured and ached after that, so she pulled her knees to her chest and stared out the long, scuffed window at the landscape whistling by.

The train passed sun-bleached hills dotted with sparse, squat houses, though for the most part, the land was sprawling and desolate. The weights in her chest shifted and settled and scratched at her like a bundle of needles. The train car was gray and the upholstery smelled just faintly of cigarettes.

Inez put her head into her hands. A soft rustling sound stirred between her ears.

She jerked up, and found bright flickers dancing in her peripheral vision. She turned to the window.

A swarm of golden petals floated astride the train, undulating like a murmuration. Inez gasped, then keened, and pressed her burnt palm to the glass.

A cluster of petals pressed back, vaguely in the shape of a hand.

See Carly Racklin's story "The Guardian of Werifest Park" online at Metaphorosis.
If you liked it, leave a comment. Authors love that!
Remember to subscribe to our e-mail updates so you'll know when new stories are posted.

About the story

The Guardian of Werifest Park might be my oldest and most revised story. A long time ago I had a dream in which a girl beckoned a giant shadowy creature out from a line of trees, fearsome to others but to her, a friend. I've always been fond of the idea of "forest spirits" or magical creatures that inhabit trees and organic things, and this story grew out of those two concepts. Almost all my stories involve forests in some way.

I fiddled with the idea for a long time, never making anything substantial of it, though never quite abandoning it either. Then, in college, with illuminating feedback from my peers and professors, I wrote the story as my senior manuscript. It went through several more transformations in the following years before it found its final home here.

In the very first draft I ever wrote of it, the story was set a rural town next to a large stretch of woods, and not a city. I like to imagine that this town is where Inez is headed at the end of the story now. Just as she starts and ends in the same place, the journey of the larger story also ends where it first began.

A question for the author

Q: Whence you do you draw inspiration for your characters?

A: My characters almost always come from little sparks of inspiration — a song, a line of dialogue that pops into my head as I'm trying to fall asleep, a picture I see while scrolling through Twitter. And of course they all carry little pieces of me in them. I think that's the spell that usually results in a character: something from me, and some bit of magic I snatch out of the world.

About the author

Carly Racklin is a storyteller, writing consultant, bird nerd, and lover of all things horror from New Jersey. She writes about monsters with hearts, monsters born from hearts, and every lovely and odd thing in-between. She possesses a B.A. in English with a concentration in Creative Writing from Arcadia University, and currently serves as an editor for Luna Station Quarterly. Her favorite birds are vultures, which she thinks more people should appreciate.

carlyracklin.com, @willowylungs

Copyright

Metaphorosis Publishing

Metaphorosis offers beautifully written science fiction and fantasy. Our projects include:

Metaphorosis Magazine

Metaphorosis, a weekly magazine of SFF short stories, including stories from all the authors in this anthology. Find out more at <u>magazine.metaphorosis.com</u>, and sign up to be notified of new stories.

Metaphorosis Books

Recent books from Metaphorosis can be found at <u>books.metaphorosis.com</u>, and include:

Score

an SFF symphony

What if stories were written like music? *Score* is an anthology of stories written to an emotional score.

Best Vegan SFF of 2018

The best vegan science fiction and fantasy stories of 2018!

Metaphorosis
2018

All the stories from *Metaphorosis* magazine's third year. Fifty-two great SFF stories.

Metaphorosis: Best of 2018

The best science fiction and fantasy stories from *Metaphorosis* magazine's third year.

Metaphorosis
2017

All the stories from *Metaphorosis* magazine's second year. Fifty-three great SFF stories.

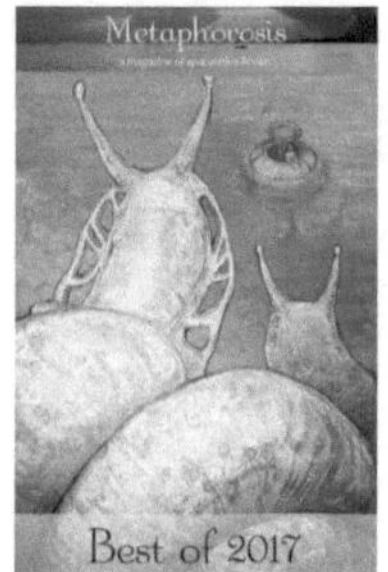

Metaphorosis:
Best of 2017

The best science fiction and fantasy stories from *Metaphorosis* magazine's *second* year.

Metaphorosis 2016

Almost all the stories from *Metaphorosis* magazine's first year.

Metaphorosis: Best of 2016

The best science fiction and fantasy stories from *Metaphorosis* magazine's first year.

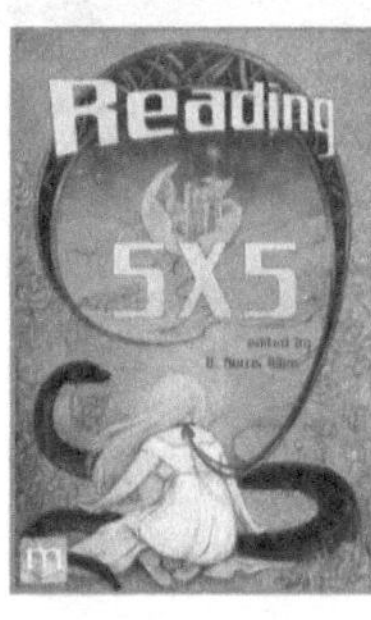 

Reading 5X5

Five stories, five times

Twenty-five SFF authors, five base stories, five versions of each – see how different writers take on the same material, with stories in contemporary and high fantasy, soft and hard SF, and a mysterious 'other' category.

Reading 5X5

Writers' Edition

All the stories from the regular, readers' edition, plus two extra stories, the story seed, and authors' notes on writing. Over 100 pages of additional material specifically aimed at writers.

Best Vegan SFF of 2017

The best vegan science fiction and fantasy stories of 2017!

Best Vegan SFF of 2016

The best vegan science fiction and fantasy stories of 2016!

Susurrus

A darkly romantic story of magic, love, and suffering.